D1155634

Spaghetti With Murder

A Terri Springe
Culinary Mystery
(with recipes)

For my friends in Antigo — S. Kay Weber

by

S. Kay Weber

Bloomington, IN   Milton Keynes, UK

authorHOUSE®

AuthorHouse™
1663 Liberty Drive, Suite 200
Bloomington, IN 47403
www.authorhouse.com
Phone: 1-800-839-8640

AuthorHouse™ UK Ltd.
500 Avebury Boulevard
Central Milton Keynes, MK9 2BE
www.authorhouse.co.uk
Phone: 08001974150

First published by AuthorHouse 9/11/2007

ISBN: 978-1-4259-4730-9 (sc)
ISBN: 978-1-4259-4731-6 (hc)

Library of Congress Control Number: 2006906607

Printed in the United States of America
Bloomington, Indiana

This book is printed on acid-free paper.

Dedication

This book is dedicated to my buddy Jesse,
who, when I told him I had always wanted to write said,
"Well, then just do it!" Thank-you, Jesse.

Acknowledgments

The author would like to acknowledge the help of the following people:

My husband and my children, for putting up with my 'first author' jitters and the constant changes to my manuscript, especially 'Beck' for her reaction to the story. My extended family, my mother and my sisters, for their support and enthusiasm.

My editor, the real J.C., one of the hardest working people, whom I have ever known.

Also, the wonderful people at the Boston Redevelopment Authority, Kellie (with an 'ie') and especially Pete Neitz, in mapping, who sent me a huge, wonderful map of the city of Boston.

The Boston Red Sox, for finally 'reversing the curse' and inspiring me, to set my story in their great city. Also, thank-you to the makers of the wonderful baseball movie, FEVER PITCH. It's all about the genuine love of the game.

All of my co-workers, who have been patiently, listening to me talk about this book, for months now.

My wonderful friends Kris, Katie, Emily, Leah and Joel, for their continuing support, encouragement and enthusiasm.

Also, thank-you to Joey Krueger, for his genuine enthusiasm, through this process and for all his help, when we needed a true friend. My nephew Levi. We would have never been able to get through the rough times without you. Also, thank-you, Larry and Dustin, for all your help.

Finally, thank-you Sarah N., to whom I still owe 'an arrangement'. Thanks for riding along Sarah.

Chapter 1

Ed Stone twirled his fork in the generous plateful of luscious spaghetti with meatballs he had served himself. "Man, that girl can really cook! I guess that's why she can make a good living at it, eh?" He laughed, for some strange reason. His dining companion looked up from a full plate, with watery eyes, too numb to answer.

"Oh, c'mon" said Ed, "how can you let this bother you? I say, let's just move forward and forget about it. It's over and done, in the past. I just needed to get it if off my chest before I die." He laughed again and continued to enjoy his meal greedily. "Hope that's O.K."

Ed was too engrossed in his food to even notice or care, that the chair was being pushed away from the other side of the table. Picking up the plate of untouched food, Ed's friend walked over to the sink to dump it into the garbage disposal, also unnoticed by Ed. Slowly, a .22 pistol was taken out of a jacket pocket. Ed's greedy way of taking everything, food, money, women, had never gone unnoticed.

"Why did I ever put up with this, *or with you? Before you die, huh?"* The words were said out loud but before Ed was able to fathom the meaning of them or become alarmed, the trigger was pulled and a bullet went through the back of his skull. Ed fell forward dead, right into his plate of spaghetti with meatballs. The killer calmly cleaned up the dishes, neatly

1

put them away into the cupboard and walked out the back door. Not with a laugh, like Ed but with sadness, bitterness and regret.

Terri Springe was up to her elbows in ground beef, onions, breadcrumbs, eggs, and her own canned tomatoes, when her cell phone screeched at her elbow.

"Oh for.....*grrrr...aaarrrrgggggh*," she griped to the empty kitchen. Then, *"Ugghh,"* Terri said, as she peeled off plastic gloves covered with gook and dropped them into the trash. She snatched up the phone and poked the talk button with a brightly polished fingernail.

"Terri's Table," she said, without looking at the caller I.D. "How may I help you?" Terri asked politely, in a business-like tone.

"Hey, Terri Springeeeeeee...." the voice on the other end sang out.

"Angie, you little bi...," Terri started to chastise her friend and was quickly interrupted.

"Now, now, is that any way to talk to your best hook-up at the cop shop?" Terri's friend, Angie teased. "Anyway, how could I resist? You usually know it's me."

"O.K., so you got me this time but you know that drives me nuts!" Terri shot back.

"Yeah, well, so drop that *dumb letter e off* the end of your last name, already," said Angie. They had this same discussion, at least a couple of times a month or so.

"Yeah, well, tell that to my birth certificate, my Social Security card, my...." Terri started going on and on, as usual.

"Blah, blah, blah," Angie cut her off again. "Wanna go to the Sox game tomorrow night?" Angie Perry was Terri's life-long, best friend. She was a short, tough, no nonsense cop at the local police station in Boston, near Terri's neighborhood and damn handy to have around, for more than one reason. Angie also had access, to *four Boston Red Sox season tickets,* which had been in her family for decades, thus giving them tickets for the World Series. Terri and Angie, along with about a zillion other loyal Red Sox fans, had freaked last year, when their team had finally won. They had been at *every* play-off game *and had put everything* on the line, to go to St. Louis and see the Sox finally win. Now that the *curse had been reversed*, the games were more fun and relaxing. Terri hadn't believed in any silly curse to start with but try telling that to the old die-hards. She still loved the games, of course, so Angie didn't need to wait long for an answer.

"Mmmm….let me think, ah, *yeah!*" Terri came back quickly, even though Angie already knew what she would say.

Actually, Terri loved all sports. She loved the Sox, the Celtics, and the Patriots…*Brady, whoa (sigh), what a doll!* At 30, single and on her own, Terri, like Angie, enjoyed her life. They had both gone through more than one unfortunate or disappointing relationship and had decided to lay off the commitment thing for awhile. It was *nice* to make decisions at the last minute. It was *nice* to not have to check in with some one else, only to do what they wanted to avoid a big discussion.

"Cool," said Angie, after Terri's positive reply. "I'll pick you up at 5:00. We'll have supper first," she decided, "some place nice, maybe Italian?"

"You'll pick me up? In the squad car? Even more cool!" Terri laughed now, good humor restored.

"Yeah, you wish," Angie laughed, too. "With the lights flashing and sirens blaring. Not likely. I'll borrow my Dad's car. He and Judith never go anywhere during the week." *Judith* was George Perry's second wife. Angie's mother, who had died from breast cancer, had been gone for eight years now but no one was more grateful than Angie, that her father had found a new person to share his life with. She missed her mom but she liked Judith and considered her more of a friend than the *step-mom* type. Terri liked her, too. She often went, with Angie, to George and Judith's modest home for lovely, delicious dinners. Judith was a marvelous cook and she loved trying new recipies and different wines with several courses. Terri and Angie often ended up spending the night, after being plied with fabulous food and wines. Terri's own parents Harvey and Emily Springe, lived in Maine, on the coast and Terri didn't make it up there as often as she would like. So visits to the Perry household, filled the bill nicely.

Terri promised to be ready for pick-up at 5:00 the next day and hit end on the phone. She snagged another pair of plastic gloves and continued with her mixing. Terri had found, the only way to thoroughly mix ground beef, with other ingredients, for meatloaf or meatballs, was with your hands. This she had learned from experience. She next grabbed two pounds of fresh ground pork, which she had picked up at her favorite butcher shop that morning. This she added to the bowl and continued to mix. Terri was making a large batch of her savory meatloaf. Along with the pork, she had also picked up the rest of her meat supplies for the week. Into her small refrigerated van, which she had procured at a police auction with Angie's help, she had loaded ten pounds of thick pork chops, three, 6-pound prime rib roasts, 20 pounds of fresh ground beef, five of which had gone into her meatloaf mixture, a dozen fryer chickens, 20 pounds of chicken breasts, two, 5-pound sticks of summer sausage and several wonderful cheeses. Also, because someone had cancelled part of an order, a beautiful, 8-pound, pork loin roast, which was in one of the ovens cooking, while she did the rest of her work. When it was done, Terri would cut the pork, into uniformed ¼ inch slices, to go with mashed potatoes, tasty gravy and a pretty combination of fresh vegetables.

Terri loved her butcher, Jack and he loved her, *professionally speaking*, of course. A family man in his forties, with three insane teenagers, he enjoyed her cheerful greeting, "Hi Jack, what's good today?"

"Everything Terri," Jack would say back, "I'm just getting your order together, now." Then he would tell her what was available, for a good price or as in the case of the pork loin roast, what someone may have backed out on, that she might be interested in. It was their routine and it had worked for nearly two years, now.

Terri hadn't moved to Boston with the intention of becoming a personal chef, it had just worked out that way. Her working space, at the moment, was the kitchen of the *Twin Pines Supper Club,* just outside of Boston. It was close enough to the city to be a short drive, *out in the country,* for customers who wanted to get away from the hustle and bustle of the city, for a couple of relaxing hours. Terri had found *Twin Pines* when, at the urging of Angie, she had first moved to the city. She was scoping out her new home and the surrounding area, when the old Ford Mustang she was driving at the time, decided to croak not far from the restaurant's parking lot and she had managed to chug to their back door. Terri had a cell phone with her back then, about five years ago, before everyone else even thought about it. Terri had carried a cell phone and a bottle of water, constantly for years now, based on her own cautious nature and her mother's paranoia. However, in this case, before calling a tow truck, curiosity made her walk in the back door of the charming, old building. There she had found two ladies who appeared to be in about their mid-fifties, drinking coffee and pouring over invoices, lists and a reservation book. A staff of about a half-dozen people gravitated around them, doing prep-work for the evening dinner crowd and delicious smells came from everywhere.

Judy and Joyce, *the twins,* as they were affectionately called by their staff, were completely different, in everyway, looks *and* personality-wise, Terri found out later. Everyone in the kitchen, had looked at Terri, as she stood by the door, not sure what to do. But when the shorter of the two women, Judy, saw her and asked, *"Honey, are you lost?"* in the kindest voice Terri could have ever imagined, she knew she had found her home away from home. They had immediately given her a cup of coffee *and* a job helping in the kitchen, *at Terri's request.* Being part of the wait-staff was just not Terri's thing. She wanted to be in the kitchen, behind the scenes, learning. It was brutal out on the floor and Terri had not the patience, nor the personality to cater to fussy customers. She liked the kitchen staff, Geoff the head cook and Dustin, second in command, were fun and easy to work with. She helped where she could with prep-work, assisting the wait-staff and the cooks, especially on week-ends, which made for busy days and hectic nights.

The two sisters had talked their rich husbands into buying the restaurant, simply because they were bored. They had raised their families and needed something to do, besides charity work. The husbands, thinking tax write-off, never imagined the two ambitious ladies would turn the beautiful, old building, into a very successful business. Week nights were steady but the week-ends were packed. The wait-staff of 25 regulars, 10 part-timers and a couple of dozen bus people, flew around taking care of customers, while the kitchen staff of six cooks and eight assistants including Terri, rushed to get the orders out and *turn* the tables at least every hour or hour and 15 minutes, *at the most*. The meals were always wholesome, delicious and beautifully presented. They also kept a rather impressive wine cellar stocked and six bartenders were kept busy from 4:30, when they opened for dinner, until about 8:30, when it started to quiet down. Terri would usually get home to her apartment by 9:30 or so, as most of the kitchen clean-up was left to the cooks and other staff.

It was in this kitchen, that Terri was now mixing her meatloaf. She patted the delicious smelling mixture of meats, breadcrumbs, spices and her canned tomatoes, into pans coated with low-fat cooking spray. She then poured cans of tomato sauce over all and placed the full pans into one of the large, pre-heated ovens.

Terri was able to use this kitchen on Mondays, when the restaurant was closed. She had gotten permission from *the twins* to use the facilities, only when she had signed an agreement, with her insistance, that the owners were not responsible for the food that went out of their establishment, for Terri's customers. Terri wasn't worried, she had complete confidence in her food. But this protected Judy and Joyce from any problems.

She prepared all the food for the six families that she cooked for, on Monday mornings. They paid her well to make home-cooked meals for their busy households. She prepared nutritious, tasty dinners for three families of five, two families of four and one family of six. Basically, she shopped for them, cooked for them, then packaged and delivered the meals, in her refrigerator truck. All families with hectic schedules, they gave her keys to their homes, so she could go in their back doors and put meals for four days, into their freezers. Usually, there was a note asking her to put one meal into the fridge for dinner that night. They left her check on the table and Terri left a sample menu for the next week. After delivering all the meals, she went straight to the bank. It was a lot of work, so Terri was already considering hiring an assistant. She also needed to can more tomatoes, soon and having someone to help, would cut her time in half.

With the meatloaf in the oven, she next mixed up a huge bowl of instant potatoes. Her families liked them, they were fast and tasted good. She then prepared gravy to go with the potatoes, meats, and several kinds of fresh vegetables, she had already steamed to put on the side. Crisp green beans, California blend, with cheese sauce and bright orange baby carrots would go well with a main course and potatoes.

The pork roast, prepared simply, with salt, pepper and rosemary, had gone into the oven as soon as she had gotten to the kitchen. It smelled fabulous when she opened the oven to check it with a meat thermometer. Terri deemed it perfectly done and removed it from the hot oven. As the pork cooled, she cut the fryers into pieces to make oven-fried chicken. After coating the chicken with flour, salt, pepper and other spices, she browned the pieces on top of the stove. She sprayed a large flat pan with cooking spray, carefully placed the browned chicken in the pan and put the pan into a hot oven. She then thoroughly washed her hands, after handling the raw chicken and put on fresh plastic gloves. She next prepared two cheese and sausage trays, a special order for one of her clients and then sliced the cooled pork.

For the last meal, she had pulled cut-up stew meat out of the big walk-in freezer from the shelf, where the sisters let her store some of her meats. She had already put the prime rib roasts, the pork chops and chicken breasts into the freezer, along with the remaining ground beef and would probably use them next week. She tried never to keep her meats frozen for more than a week. Terri did everything she could, to have the freshest food possible but to save time and money, she sometimes had to buy ahead. She proceeded to make a big batch of beef stew, for the fourth meal. With the stew, the family could have a salad and rolls, perhaps with a pie or cake for dessert, picked up on the way home. That way, they had their complete meal and everyone was happy. There were no fussy eaters in Terri's clientel, they all loved her food, kids and grown-ups alike.

Terri was almost done cleaning up and getting ready to load her van, when her phone chirped again. This time she did check the caller I.D. and saw that it was Angie calling back. She hit the talk button and without a greeting said, "What, did you loose the tickets or something?'

"Aaaaah, Terri," Angie sounded grim and professional, "I have some bad news."

Terri's stomach dropped, "Angie, what...?" She managed to get out only two words, before Angie went on.

"Some neighbors found your old buddy Ed Stone, dead in his kitchen about 30 minutes ago. He..."

Terri interrupted Angie assuming, since Ed was 75 years old and had smoked and drank most of his life, that it was natural causes. "Oh, that's too bad," she said, tears stinging her eyes, "did he go quickly?"

"Oh yeah, " Angie said, in a strange voice, "it was quick alright. Not only was he dead but they found him face down in a plate of your spaghetti with meatballs!" Before Terri could absorb that bizarre fact, Angie finished her report.

"Terri," she said, "he was shot at close range, in the back of the head, with a .22 pistol."

Chapter 2

There is *never* a good reason to be in a cemetery. Terri was sure of that, as she stared at Ed's fresh grave, in the Westerly Burying Ground, in West Roxbury. Oh, maybe you might come to look up old relatives or visit the grave of a loved one but it always meant, *someone had died.* It's like that old joke, *Hey, how many people in this cemetery are dead? Uh,...all of them, silly!'* Well, ha,ha, thought Terri.

Who had shot Ed and why? The last three days had gone by in a blur and now Terri was standing by the pile of dirt, where Ed was six feet under, contemplating these questions. She was convinced, that it was someone who knew him well. She had argued with Angie about it.

"Angie, I know how much food I had taken over to Ed that afternoon. There was more than enough for two meals *or* for two people. What happened to the rest of the spaghetti?" Terri begged her friend to listen.

"Terri, I know how you feel but there was no evidence to show, that someone was eating there with Ed *and* there is no way for you to prove how much food you took over there," Angie stated firmly.

"That's not fair and you know it." Terri was shaking, she was so frustrated.

"I can't deal with what's fair and *you* know it," Angie softened her tone, trying to calm her friend. "We can only deal with hard evidence. I also realize, that you are upset because Ed ended up face down in a plate of your spaghetti with meatballs, *after* someone plugged him in the back of the noggin,' " she quipped.

"Angie!" Terri was at the breaking point. "How can you be so insensitive?"

"*Terri!*" Angie mimicked her, as she spouted back. "Why are you having such a fit? You didn't even like the guy all that much."

"Yeah, O.K., well obviously I'm not real happy that Ed fell into a plate of my food but he was a regular customer at *Twin Pines* and poor Cal is devastated."

Cal Johnson was Ed's best friend and he was almost inconsolable at the loss of his old buddy. They had done everything together. School, Korea, families, a whole lifetime of experiences and Cal just kept saying over and over, "*He was my best friend. I still can't believe it. He was my best friend.*"

Terri was convinced Cal would also die soon, now that his old buddy was gone. Cal himself, had heart problems and certainly this murder had been very stressful on his health and well-being. Terri and Angie had tried to talk to Cal, to see if he had any ideas, on who may have committed the murder. There had always been rumors that Ed kept lots of cash in his house.

"*Don' t like banks,*" he had always said. Cal said that wasn't true, however. Ed just pretended he had money. It made him feel better, since he had lost most of his savings years ago gambling and spending recklessly.

"Why would there be any money?" Cal had asked tearfully. "Most people didn't know it but as soon as Ed got his Social Security or pension checks, he'd just go out and fritter it all away," Cal finished, sadly. Then he just looked down at the old, wrinkled handkerchief in his hands and seemed no longer able to talk about it.

"Now there's a word you don't hear every day of the week," commented Angie, under her breath, to Terri, "*fritter.*" Then, realizing they were getting no where, she gave-up trying to ask Cal any more questions. "Mmmmm, well O.K., Cal old buddy," Angie said, " you just take it easy and we'll talk later." Then they left him to his mourning.

There had been a small group at the funeral. Judy and Joyce, a few neighbors and what was left of the local Korean War contingent. In their ill-fitting uniforms but *oh, how they loved them*, with hats perched on bald or gray heads, the Veterans, made up a good third of the mourners. Also, Terri, Angie and Cal, who sat behind Ed's niece and nephew, the only relatives who had bothered to show up. Ed had very few relation, Cal explained. There had only been one brother and he had died some time ago. Ed had no children of his own, even though he had been married twice. His first wife had died. His second wife had left him and they had been divorced ten years ago. Terri suspected, the niece and nephew had showed up, hoping there was money to claim. Obviously, that was not the case, so they would probably sell the house and it's contents, which also didn't amount to much and that would be it. *Except*, thought Terri, *someone would still need to find out who had murdered Ed.* Angie hadn't been very certain about how far they would go with the investigation. The rumors were flying like crazy. However, the police department seemed to feel, with Ed's gambling problem and no money, that a couple of heavies had walked in the back door, demanded their money and shot Ed, execution style, when he wouldn't or couldn't, hand it over. Terri of course, was livid with this conclusion but she wasn't going to deal with it now.

At the moment, Terri was focused on two totally unexpected guests at the funeral. They were Cal's daughter, Elizabeth and *her daughter,* Cal's grandaughter, Brianna. Brianna looked fine but Elizabeth, Terri was not so sure about. Something was very strange. Even though Ed had been Cal's best friend all their lives, Elizabeth was not there to grieve. On the contrary, she was holding back some other strong emotion and Terri suspected that it was anger. Terri felt she just had to talk to Elizabeth and find out what was going on with her. If Elizabeth, as Terri was thinking, was totally pissed-off about something, *why and what was she even doing at this funeral?*

Terri looked over at her and at that moment, Elizabeth looked up and met Terri's eyes. Terri gave her a questioning look back but suddenly, Elizabeth forced herself to make her face go completely blank. Terri was very confused. They had met briefly before the funeral and she had seemed nice enough. *What was up, anyway?* Terri would have to chase her down later and try to find out what her problem was.

The service, to Terri's relief, was held grave side. Big, old churches made her edgy and uncomfortable. One of the veterans, an army chaplain, had said a few words, keeping the ceremony short, much to *everyone's* relief. Also, Terri was glad there had been no viewing of the body. She *could not* get the picture of a dead Ed, face down in her spaghetti with meatballs, out of her mind. *Of course, it wasn't like there were still bits of pasta and sauce still stuck to his face. They would have cleaned him up, wouldn't they? Well, wouldn't they?*

"Stop it!" Terri said, in a stage whisper, putting her hand to her throbbing forehead.

"No, you stop it!" said Angie, giving her a goofy look.

"Angie, don't start," whispered Terri back at her, "my head is about to explode!"

"Well, if it does," said Angie, quietly, "I'm not cleaning it up!"

What was that, cop talk? Terri choked on a giggle starting in her throat but managed to gain some semblance of control by placing a handkerchief over her mouth. This motion on her part, made it appear as if she were muffling a sob, forcing all in attendance to look at her sympathetically. Terri coughed delicately and looked down. She couldn't wait to get out of there!

Mercifully, the service was quickly over. They had all trekked out to the plot where Ed was buried for the small memorial observance but when one of the Korean War vets, started to play *Taps,* Angie and Terri both almost lost it. As soon as he was done, Angie grabbed Terri's arm.

"Let's get out of here," Angie said, as she dragged Terri away from the grave site. "Cemetaries give me the heebie-geebies!" Terri looked back at Elizabeth Johnson, or rather Severson, which was her married name.

"But I need to talk to Cal's daughter!" Terri protested, trying to release herself from Angie's grip.

"Cal's daughter? Why?" Angie needed a stiff drink, *she needed it now* and she was losing patience with her friend.

"She knows something, I can tell, I don't know, I......," Terri put her hand to her forehead again. *She had the worst headache of her life!*

"Terri, snap out of it!" Angie hissed, shaking her pal, none too gently. "Let's get back to Twin Pines. I need a martini and I want to get out of this stupid, creepy, cemetery *right now!* I took the day off for this funeral. I missed my Sox game this week....."Angie continued to drag Terri away and toward the car.

"Sox game....." Terri parroted, feeling like she was floating off into space. *All of it had been just way too much for her to digest.*

"Oh, get into the car." Angie finally gave up trying to reason with her spacey friend, as they reached her Dad's Buick Regal. She opened the car door on the passenger side, shoved Terri in and shut the door. Angie often showed amazing strength under duress, which was one of the things, that made her a good police officer. She was using that strength now. Angie got in and started the car, which immediately began making annoying but effective, beeping noises, to alert passengers to buckle their seat belts. The sound seemed to help Terri come back down to earth. She grabbed her belt to buckle it into place, as they took off, away from the cemetery and Ed's final resting place.

"Take it easy, Terri," Angie said more calmly now, "I heard Cal say, that Elizabeth and Brianna are going to stay with him for a couple of days. You'll probably be able to catch up with them at Cal's house, sometime before they leave."

Terri registered this and acknowledged that she could use some refreshment herself, liquid or otherwise. A buffet luncheon had been planned at the *Twin Pines*, for after the funeral. Maybe Elizabeth and Brianna would attend with Cal and Terri could talk with her there.

Judy and Joyce, had instructed the staff to set up a nice assortment of food, buffet style. It was ready when the group from the memorial service arrived. There were ham and chicken salad sandwiches and an assortment of cheeses, beautifully arranged on elaborate, silver trays. It was from Judy, that Terri had learned to put together, attractive arrangements of cheese, meats, fresh vegetables, or fruits, whatever the occasion or client called for and that professionalism showed, for this event. There were also, tangy deviled eggs, two beautiful pasta salads and the *Twin Pines,*' famous potato salad and cole slaw. Also, on the buffet, were pretty bowls of chips, pickles, and olives, along with a large pot of coffee, bubbling at the end of the table. Glass plates, coffee cups and nice flatware, had been placed at the beginning of the spread, along with napkins, mints and assorted nuts. Not many of the group, wanted coffee however, as most bellied up to the bar, including Angie and Terri.

Angie gratefully accepted and began sipping a martini, with three huge cocktail olives, soaking in the strong drink of gin and vermouth. Terri opted for a strawberry margarita. She enjoyed a good white wine with dinner, now and then but wine often just made her tired. Terri was a wimp when it came to alcohol and she admitted it freely. Right now, the margarita was cool and refreshing, perfect for a warm August day. Terri leaned over the bar and grabbed a couple more lime slices to float in her drink from the bar carousel, full of bright fruits and pickled veggies.

"Hey, Terri," Brenda chided her with a wink, "stop snaggin' my bar goodies!"

"Thanks Brenda," said Terri, giving her a wicked grin. Brenda, the bar-tender on site for the funeral luncheon, was serving the Korean War Vets, who were imbibing with vigor. Brenda was short and tough, like Angie and Terri liked her a lot. As for the Vets, any serious funeral nonsense had disappeared quickly. They had immediately filled their plates from the food tables and had taken them to the bar, for cold beer to go with their lunch. The meal was donated by Judy and Joyce but everyone was on their own at the bar, so the Vets were sticking with the less expensive drink. They laughed and joked and told old stories, as people from that generation tend to do. Even Cal seemed to be enjoying himself, as he nibbled on a ham sandwich and took a healthy drink of cold beer.

Terri, on the other hand, sighed deliberately more loudly than she should have, to get Angie's attention.

"Now what?" Angie asked, impatient again but a bit more relaxed as she sipped her precious drink and bit into a pickle. *That,* as it turned out, *was a mistake!* Angie's face puckered up like an old prune and she almost spit out pickle and drink. Terri saw her and started to laugh. She needed to, after the last couple of days. Angie's face was *beyond hysterical* for funny. When Terri finally got a hold of herself and took a breath from laughing, she asked, "What happened? Why would a dill pickle with a martini, be any different than an olive with a martini?"

"It isn't dill," Angie managed to get out, "it's *sweet!* When you bite into a pickle, expecting dill and get sweet...."she was trying to recover from her ordeal with the offending pickle, in dramatic fashion.

"I get the picture. Gimme that." Terri snatched the rest of the bright green, sweet pickle away from Angie, as she saw her move to throw it into the trash. Terri crunched on the rest of the pickle. Angie quickly took a forkful of the wonderful potato salad, another sip of her martini, and another bite of potato salad. Finally regaining her composure, Angie looked at Terri.

"O.K., so after all that nonsense, what was all the heavy sighing about?" Angie asked, rolling her eyes.

"Well, Elizabeth isn't here," Terri pouted, trying to regain her composure. "I really need to talk to her."

"Terri," Angie said, more than a little impatient again, "why would she be here? She doesn't know anybody and what in the hell makes you think that whatever is on her mind, has *anything* to do with Ed's murder?"

"I'm not sure. There was just *something*......," Terri just couldn't get past the look, she had seen on Elizabeth's face at the funeral service.

"Well, she and Brianna will be staying with Cal for a couple of days. Call over there or stop by and see if Elizabeth will talk to you. Whatever is on her mind, like I said, it probably has *nothing whatsoever*, to do with this case. No matter what, she may not want to talk to anyone about it. She might just tell you to mind your own business. Or she might just tell you to butt out. Then you'll be disappointed, so be ready for that." Angie warned, as she popped a booze soaked olive into her mouth and savored it. "Oh, yummy," she cooed and rolled her eyes again, this time with pleasure, "much, much better."

"Yeah, well *thanks* for the vote of confidence, pal," Terri said, as she watched her friend, who seemed to be enjoying herself immensely.

Angie ignored this and said, thinking now. "Hey, do you think *the twins* would let me leave my dad's Regal in their parking lot over night?"

"Why?" Terri smirked. "You planning on getting plastered?"

"No, not plastered, just relaxed. Besides, you know the rules and *I am* an officer of the law, after all," Angie said, importantly.

Terri was not impressed but she and Angie were on the same page with drinking and driving. Terri and Angie were not big drinkers anymore. They had gone through that phase a decade ago, in college. However, any amount of alcohol could make, *even the best driver,* unable to drive safely, so a taxi would be their mode of transportation home for this afternoon.

"I'm sure you can leave your Dad's car here without a problem. How will you get it back then?" Terri wondered.

"One of my buddies at the cop shop will drive me back tomorrow after my shift." That settled, Angie slid off her bar stool. "I need some more food," she said, "and why haven't you gotten something yourself? Everything is marvelous." Angie moved over to the table to see what was left and Terri followed her, picking up a plate, napkin and fork.

"Best chicken salad in the world," Terri said, as she picked up a sandwich, a couple of pieces of cheese, a pickle, dill this time, a scoop of potato salad and one of coleslaw. "I forgot, I haven't eaten much in the last couple of days," Terri said, as they headed back to their drinks. "Mmmm," Terri swooned, as she chewed a bite of sandwich. "I'm famished and this is just what the doctor ordered." She took a forkful of the creamy potato salad.

Angie watched her, amused. "No wonder you're so *damn skinny*," she observed, "eat one day, don't eat three days."

"Angie, *I am not skinny!*" Terri protested. "Anyway, *not eating* is the worst thing you can do, if you're worried about your weight. We both know that. I don't eat a lot when I'm upset about something and the last three days have been very upsetting and weird, to say the least. Besides, I gained three pounds last week so I gotta watch it." She took another bite of sandwich and chewed thoughtfully.

"Oh, *boo-hoo!*" said Angie who, at five feet, four inches tall, was constantly battling her weight. She had to stay fit for her job, so she was always on some new diet, to lose 10 pounds and strain to keep it off.

Terri was O.K. with her weight. She liked the way she looked in her jeans and slim skirts but she swore that if she gained an ounce, she could feel it in the way her clothes fit. When Terri looked in the mirror, she never felt satisfied. Not gorgeous but certainly not unattractive, she just always felt so, well.....*ordinary*. She had felt that way all her life and saw no reason to change that opinion, this late in the game. She knew a lot of extremely attractive people but if they had a lousy, selfish personality, it didn't matter what they looked like. The media didn't help either. With shampoo and make-up ads on television and in magazines, it seemed as if everyone was supposed to look like Tyra Banks or Heidi Klum, with perfect skin and gorgeous, flowing locks of shiny hair. Terri kept her light, unremarkable brown hair, short, usually cut around her ears. Fortunately, it was thick and healthy, with enough body so she could shower, blow it dry and after putting on a minimal amount of make-up, throw on her clothes and split. Terri was just too busy for anything more.

She and Angie finished their food and drinks, three for Angie, just two for Terri. They said good-bye to Cal and were reassured, that his buddies would look after him and see him safely home, where Elizabeth and Brianna would be waiting for him. They also thanked *the twins* and made sure they knew, Angie would be leaving her dad's car, parked in their lot overnight. Angie and Terri, had already called for their taxi, which would drop them off at their respective apartments on Corey St. The girls, only lived about two blocks apart but had decided on separate abodes, since they both led such hectic lives.

"I'll call you tomorrow," said a sleepy Angie, "we'll try to catch a game over the week-end, K.?" Terri, who had been dropped off first, said fine and climbed the flight of stairs on the outside of the building, to her front door.

When Terri unlocked the door of her cozy, four room apartment, she knew who would be waiting for her on the other side. Terri's two cats, Maria and Louie, were pretty much the poofiest kitties you could ever imagine. A brother and sister, spade and neutered, of course, they were of the seal-point variety, with brown markings on the ears, feet, tails and faces. Since however, *daddy* was a pure-bred Persian, they were fluffy to the extreme. They were also *very* friendly, *very* demanding and *very* naughty, especially when they were bored. Not satisfied with just each other for company, they seemed to get into all kinds of trouble if Terri neglected them for more than a day.

Right now, they greeted her enthusiastically. Maria, the smaller of the two, sang her hello in a series of soft, delicate mews. Louie, her much bigger brother, made his welcome a little louder, as they both vied for her attention. Terri tripped over them as she shut the door, locked it and threw her keys and small hand-bag, on a hall table to the right of the door. She bent down and tried to give them both attention at the same time. She felt guilty for not spending more quality time with them in the last couple of days. What with Ed's murder, trying to do her work and get to a couple of marketing classes she was taking on Tuesday and Wednesday mornings, then the funeral on this Wednesday afternoon, Terri had spent little time with the furry felines. However, as she looked up to survey the great room of her apartment, which was kitchen and living room, separated by a peninsula counter with bar stools around it, Terri's eyes came to rest on the havoc wreaked by the busy pair.

"What the....?" she exclaimed, as she saw what they had done. The one thing in abundance, in Terri's apartment, were books. These many books, on several different subjects, were neatly arranged in a half-dozen book cases of various sizes. One of the cases was in the corner of the kitchen area and it seemed her two pets, had decided to empty it's contents. Every single book, most of them cookbooks, hence a book case in the kitchen, had been dumped on to the floor. They had also gotten up on top of the case and thrown three baskets, that normally sat up there, also on to the floor. Kitchen needs such as hot pads, small utensils, random recipes and coupons cut from newspapers and magazines, along with other assorted odds and ends, were scattered all over the place.

"Oh, man," Terri hollered at the two, "thanks a lot, you guys! This is how you repay me for food, shelter, love..... *aaaarrgggghhhh!!!!*"

She ran to the mess and got down on her hands and knees, to sort through the pile and make some sense of it. This was not to be. The two beasts jumped on her *and* the mess, not helping, only hindering, until she finally gave up. She pushed them out of the way and crawled, since she was still on the floor, to the drawer where she kept their food. Fresh food would hopefully distract the pair long enough for her to clean up after them.

"Geez, you two are worse than kids!" Terri scolded them, like they cared one way or another. "Although, if you were kids, I could leave you with a sitter and they would have to clean up after you." Louie and Maria, still weren't listening, just dancing around her with happiness, that she was home.

Terri took their bag of food out of the drawer where she stored it, since the two felines, had yet to figure out how to open a drawer. She wondered when that day would come. They had pretty much gotten into everything else. They really were almost like two little kids. What one didn't think of, the other one did, so they were *always* up to something. Still, they were her babies and as Terri filled their dishes and water bowls, she forgave them immediately, as usual. Cats were cats but they really were low maintenance and good company. Terri loved dogs, too. Her beloved Yellow Lab, Bud, was with her parents. She just didn't have the time or the patience to walk a dog and the idea of carrying a tiny mutt in a bag, ala' Paris Hilton, was ridiculous and definitely not her style. *Where did a dog like that pee and poop?* She had always wondered. Did these people have some flunky follow them around, hand them the bag once in awhile and say, *"Hey, could you clean out my purse? Oh, and while your at it, find my lip gloss and Visa card?"* Oh well. She'd rather put up with Maria and Louie. Made much more sense. Right now, they buried their faces in bowls of kitty nibble, while she straightened up the mess. That done, she washed her face and changed into her jammies.

Suddenly, she felt hungry herself, having not eaten that much at the funeral luncheon. She dug into the fridge for a late supper with T.V., before bed. Maria and Louie, were never *really* hungry and certainly didn't need people food but they were always interested in what Terri was having. After perusing the contents of the fridge, she came up with cold, fried chicken, her favorite. She always made extra to take home, after cooking for her clients. With it she had a scoop of pasta salad, sent home with her, by Judy and several small pieces of good aged, sharp cheddar, also her favorite. Along with a glass of White Zinfandel, Terri had her supper.

She settled in on her comfy sofa, a pale green sectional, covered with throw pillows and afghans. She had purchased it, along with several other pieces of furniture, at a moving sale found by Angie, to fill her apartment when she had first come to Boston. Terri had also bought a love seat, a desk, the bar stools, a bedroom set and a couple of her book cases, at the same sale. Angie had borrowed a pick-up truck from one of her work mates and just like that, Terri had furnished her new digs. Other things had eventually followed. More book cases, random knick-knacks, more books, all found at yard or tag sales. The bargains were out there, you just had to look for them.

The cats settled in with her, one on each side, sniffing politely as she ate her meal and watched an old episode of *Frasier*. Finally, supper over, fatigue overtook her and Terri crawled into bed. Maria and Louie settled down at her feet. They usually had to take at least a half an hour or so to groom themselves, sometimes even washing each others faces, while Terri read a novel or the Boston Globe. Tonight however, *she was just too beat*. She *knew* she had to try to find out what had happened and why someone would murder Ed. Terri also wanted to do what she could, to help Cal deal with his grief but she couldn't do anything, *not anymore tonight*. As soon as she shut off the light, the cats settled in and Terri zonked.

Chapter 3

So it was Thursday, the day after the funeral, that Terri stood in a shaded corner of the cemetery, staring at the pile of dirt that was Ed's grave. There would be no marker for awhile of course, only a small wire stand with the name of the deceased, the date of birth and the date of death printed on it.

EDWARD JAMES STONE
BORN: 12-17-29
DIED: 08-07-2005

Some of Ed's old Army buddies had decided to pitch in for a small headstone. It seemed a given that his niece and nephew could have cared less. *What a shame*, Terri thought as she stared at the fresh grave. *He must have been awfully lonely.* Granted, judging from his personality and choice of lifestyle, he probably had never been the easiest person in the world to live with. As a matter of fact, his choice of lifestyle, presumably the gambling, may have even been the reason for his untimely demise. He definitely had made some very bad choices. So in the end, if Ed was lonely, he had more than likely brought it on himself. Still, Terri couldn't deal with the fact, that his murder may never be solved. *Whoever had done this, should not be allowed to just walk away from it, free as a bird. Someone had to be responsible and someone had to know something. Someone had to be brought to justice.*

Terri, at least for Cal's sake, was determined to do whatever it took to figure it out. She had always been a cautious person and had no desire to mess with a bunch of *gangsters*, for lack of a better word. On the other hand, there shouldn't be much real danger just asking the neighbors or some of his old cronies, a few questions. Also, there was still Elizabeth to consider. It seemed unlikely but Terri just could not shake the weird feeling, that there was some bizarre connection going on there. Elizabeth was angry, *very angry* about something and *it had to do with Ed.* Terri's instincts told her that and up to this point, her instincts had usually been right!

"Who shot you, Ed?" Terri asked the words out loud. "Did you piss someone off, steal someone's woman?" Highly unlikely, for a man who was 75 years old, but these days, you never know. Terri did not believe dead people could hear anything, much less answer a person back, so she nearly jumped out of her skin when someone spoke at her elbow.

"Ahhhhh!!!" Terri yelled and backed up, nearly tripping over the loose dirt around the grave. "What the......ah...., *who the hell are you?*" Terri gasped rudely, mostly because he had scared the daylights out of her and *was Terri glad that it was daylight, the way her heart was pounding.* At least it wasn't dark and foggy, like some cheesy, teen slasher movie. No, it was the middle of the afternoon and the person who had spoken looked pretty normal. The man, of indeterminate age, wearing grundgy clothes, holding a shovel and laughing, repeated the question he had asked her.

"You don't really expect the guy to answer, do you?" he asked with a grin on a face that definitely could use a shave.

"No, I don't but....*who are you?*" Terri asked a little more calmly this time, as she backed up a little more.

"I'm Pete Richards, the caretaker here, girlie," he said with another grin, this time showing crooked and missing teeth.

Girlie? You have got to be kidding, Terri thought and then, *did he say his name was Keith Richards?* Out loud, she said, "So what, you just go around scaring the crap out of people for kicks? Oh and what's with the shovel? Don't tell me you actually dig graves?" Terri sounded braver than she was, as she brushed invisible dirt off her jeans to steady her shaking hands. *Pete Richards,* he said his name was, *Pete Richards.*

"Naw, I don't dig graves, machines do these days," *Pete* was still laughing at her, "and yeah, I suppose I do go around scaring the crap out of people just for kicks. You gotta admit, it's kind of funny and it gets pretty boring around here. Someone has to be awake to keep an eye on things. He sure isn't," Pete said, pointing to Ed's grave, "shot in the back of the head, I heard."

"Yeah, well," Terri had determined by this time, that Pete, the caretaker, was pretty harmless, "you heard right."

"So, you a friend of his or what?" Pete asked still amused and obviously more than a little curious about the murder.

"More like a friend of a friend," Terri answered cryptically, "and no one seems to have any clue why someone would shoot an old man in the back of the head. I was just here to think, that's all," she said, defending her right to stand in a creepy cemetery, in broad daylight and talk to a grave.

"Well, I guess I'd better get going, got lots to do. It was nice to meet you, Pete. My name is Terri Springe. You probably saw my truck over there. I'm a chef, so I'd better get back to my work."

Pete, however, had pretty much lost interest by now, so he waved a bored good-bye and took off toward a small storage shed where a riding lawn mower sat. Terri went to her truck, got in the front seat and leaned her head on the steering wheel knowing what she needed to do next. *She needed to go to Ed's house.*

Chapter 4

Terri turned left out of the cemetery and headed towards Ed's house. It was only a couple of blocks away near a mobile home park, so she didn't have far to drive. Angie would have a fit if she new what Terri was doing. She wondered if the yellow crime tape was still around the place but she didn't have to wonder long. As she drove up to the house, Terri saw it was still surrounded by the police ribbon, warning any who dared, not to cross into the marked off crime area.

The house itself really wasn't much to look at. It was a mobile home but an extra room and a lean-too had been built on, to make it a bit larger for the young family that had lived there before Ed. Terri drove around to the door that led into the kitchen area, where she had been just a few days ago, when she had dropped the spaghetti off for Ed's supper, last Sunday evening. Instead of finishing his dinner however, Ed had ended up face down in it and Terri just could not shake the thought of that bizarre scene. Anyone who may have come in the back door, probably would not have been seen, as the back door, of the small abode did not face the street or other houses. Terri could figure that much out for herself. Still, she figured it wouldn't hurt to ask the neighbors a couple of questions, anyway. The police of course, would have already questioned everyone but most people had a tendency not to tell the cops, things they might tell regular people. Mostly out of fear, Angie had told her, especially if it involves a murder investigation.

Terri ducked under the tape and went in cautiously, discovering the door was not locked, as usual. The place reeked of stale cigarette smoke and Terri felt her senses assaulted. She clutched her stomach and looked around. The kitchen wasn't much. Just a table and chairs, refrigerator, sink and counter tops, with a few cupboards. All the floors in the place were covered with a dreadful, cheap, hunter green carpet, worn pretty thin over the years. It certainly needed vacuuming, with all the people that had tramped through in the last couple of days but Terri was in no mood for house work. She looked around the kitchen, trying to figure out just what she thought she was going to find. She looked in the fridge and sure enough, there was no more spaghetti left and the container, a disposable aluminum flat pan, had disappeared completely. *Ah, ha*, she thought, *check the garbage!* Two things to keep in mind when you are looking for clues, *check the garbage and look for anything that seems to be out of place.* She wasn't sure where she had learned this but it seemed to make good sense.

Terri always took any food, she delivered to her customers or to friends, in recyclable aluminum or plastic, containers. It saved time and trouble for everyone. That being the case, the container should at least be here. She looked under the sink to check the garbage, excited to maybe find *anything* to back up her theory but she was disappointed. The garbage had been emptied and a new bag had been put into place.

"*What?*" she said out loud once again, talking to no one but herself, "*I can't believe this! Damn it!*" Terri threw the empty garbage can back under the sink and slammed the cupboard door. She opened the cabinet where Ed had kept plates and coffee cups. His dinner plates were the old, blue flowered pattern of Corning Ware, from the 70's. Terri knew this because her mom still had some exactly like them, even though she had bought several other sets of dishes since then. Some people just couldn't stand to get rid of anything, that was her mom and dad.

Ed, on the other hand, didn't have much of anything left in the small place he had called home. Terri observed this fact, after looking at the plates and seeing nothing, that looked like any kind of evidence. What appeared to be a small amount of sauce on the top plate, could have been anything. There were only five plates left in the stack. The one Ed had fallen into, had been broken, Angie had reported to Terri.

The living room area, where Ed had watched T.V., smoked, or whatever, had very little furniture in it. An old recliner, that wasn't in very good shape, faced the old television. There was a small table next to the chair with a lamp on it, an ash tray, a T.V. Guide and some candy wrappers. Pretty random stuff, for an old guy who didn't do much when he wasn't gambling and wasting money. Terri remembered that Ed used to have some really nice pieces of furniture in the place. There had been, what appeared to be an old hutch and buffet, that may have been worth some money. There had also been a couple of chairs, covered with what Terri would have called chintz. They had also appeared to be old. Also missing, were several vases, bowls and other collectables, that had been in the hutch. Had Ed sold all these pieces to pay gambling debts? It was a well-known con game. Dishonest people, who called themselves *antique dealers*, went to the homes of older people and gave them little or nothing for their old pieces of furniture. When senior citizens were desperate for money, any cash looked good and they were duped into taking what they could get.

These thoughts were going through Terri's mind, when she looked down next to the lamp table and saw a wooden magazine holder. Next to it were pieces of the Sunday Boston Globe, sorted into a couple of piles. In the holder were a couple of hunting magazines and strangely enough, a *Beckett Baseball Card Monthly* price guide. Terri had seen this magazine many times, since her brother Rob was a sports card enthusiast. He collected, sold and traded cards on the internet, with a sports card website. Her brother Rob was twenty-eight years old. What was a 75 year old man doing buying a baseball card magazine? Terri had never heard Ed talk about sports cards, *ever.* Not that she hung out with him all that much but it seemed a bit strange. As Terri looked through the magazine holder she realized, not only was the magazine in the house but Ed *subscribed* to the publication. His address was printed on a label and stuck to the cover of the August issue. Closer examination of the rack, showed it also contained issues from June and July. Terri felt more surprised then if she had found publications containing naked women in them. Considering Ed's personality, that would have made more sense. It would have been *gross* but it would have definitely made more sense. Was this the *something out of place* she was looking for? Terri wasn't sure yet but she figured she'd better get out of there pretty quick. Since the back door had not been locked, she couldn't be charged with breaking and entering but it was still a crime scene.

Aside from the small bathroom, there was only the bedroom. That also, was not a very big room. It did however, boast a rather nice bedroom set, apparently the only furniture Ed felt he needed to hang on to. The bed was old-fashioned, with dark brown wooden head and foot boards, the kind with big, heavy posts. The dresser matched and had very little on it, save a lamp, some assorted socks, handkerchiefs, another ash tray, of course, and *an old baseball trophy?* What in the world was this? Perhaps that odd, *even more out of place thing* she might be looking for? Terri picked up the trophy and looked at it. It didn't have anyone's name on it, just said 2nd place in some old tournament from days gone by and the year, 1953. It certainly was of no value whatsoever, that Terri could see but something made her turn it upside down and look at the bottom. Maybe it was the size of the base on which the little tarnished player holding the bat, was standing. It was almost exactly the size of a baseball card but a tad bigger. *Just enough*, as it turned out. The old piece of purple felt on the bottom was loose in one corner, so Terri pulled at it, just a little. There was a card in there and Terri almost screamed when she saw it. She held it in her hands reverently, looking at the bright blue background of the photo. It was in very good condition and was encased in a clear plastic sleeve. Tears came to Terri's eyes as she looked at the youthful face, the New York Yankees baseball cap, the bat over the right shoulder. In her hand, Terri held a 1952 Topps, New York Yankees baseball trading card containing a picture of the great *Mickey Mantle*. It was *the rookie card of all rookie cards* and Terri *knew* this one was genuine. Terri could only guess at it's value. She also knew, sports cards, as they were graded according to their condition, took on different numbers, from 10 on down, thus determining the worth of each individual card.

Right now, Terri just couldn't believe what she was looking at. Had Ed had this card all these years? Had he acquired it new, out of a pack with a piece of gum in it and for some odd reason, kept it and took care of it? Why? How could anyone have known back then? The card was in *almost* perfect condition, judging from what Terri had seen of the cards Rob had sealed in plastic cases. *This card should be in a museum!* Just thinking about her brother's reaction if he saw this card, made Terri dizzy.

Terri knew, *she should get the hell out of there* and head right to the police station to show the card to Angie but she just couldn't stop staring at it. *Suddenly, her mind was made up for her.* She felt a push from behind, as someone put an elbow into her back. Terri was forced forward so hard, that she lunged, knocking the breath out of her lungs and banging her head on one of the heavy wooden posts, at the top of the bed. The card went flying out of her hand but she stayed conscious, long enough to realize that someone must have been hiding in the small closet. After that, the last thing she remembered was sliding to the floor and hearing running footsteps, as her assailant made away with the precious card.

Chapter 5

Terri reached up and touched the bump on her forehead. Something had roused her into a fuzzy consciousness. *What was it? Tolling bells? A smoke alarm?* She couldn't think and then the sound stopped. She rested until it started again and finally realized it was her cell phone. She took it out of her pocket and answered with a subdued, "Yes?" and went on to say a more emphatic, *"Owww!"*, as her head started to throb from the bump and the effort it took to move.

"Terri!" screamed Angie, making Terri move the phone as far from her ear as strength would allow. "Terri, *where in the hell are you?* I've been trying to get a hold of you for an hour. You said, *owww,* where are you? What is going on?"

Angie had gone off on a panicked tirade of questions, she wouldn't stop asking long enough for Terri to answer. Terri, who was almost sure she was suffering from a slight concussion at the very least, didn't know which question to even consider, so she started with the first one.

"I'm at Ed's house. I just wanted to look around...." Terri managed to get out, before Angie went totally nuts on her.

"Are you out of your mind?" Angie was beyond livid and shock. *"That is a crime scene. What in the hell are you thinking?"*

"Angie, stop!" Terri tried to yell over her and her tone of voice must have gotten through to her friend because Angie finally took a breath, so that Terri could get out her next thought.

"Someone was here, in the closet. They came out and pushed me from behind. I hit my head on the bed post and I think I may have a concussion, I...." That was as far as she got.

"Terri," Angie was now understandably alarmed. She said two words and tried to sound as firm as possible. *"Don't move!"*

Terri heard the two words but chose to listen to only one of them and that was, *move!* She got up the best she could, stumbled a bit and tried to move along, hanging on to the grubby walls, for support. She just had to get out of this stuffy, little dump and get some air. All of the sudden, Terri was overcome from the stench of cigarette smoke. She felt like she was going to throw-up. *She knew she was going to throw-up!* Terri fell out the door, on to the grass and started to retch. She could hear sirens in the distance and came to realize someone standing above her, had put a hand on her back for comfort. Terri tensed in fear but then looked up into the kind face of Gina Maclaughlin, Ed's neighbor. She was a *very* nice lady and Terri was *so* glad to see her. She leaned against Gina for comfort and support.

"Terri," Gina's voice was kind and soothing, "it's O.K., Honey, get it out. You've gone through an ordeal and help is on the way."

Terri had stopped vomiting by then. As usual, she hadn't eaten much that day but it was still early. Mostly, she was just choking from the nausea coming from the pain in her head. The sound of the approaching sirens wasn't helping either but at least it made her feel like she was going to be alright. Angie was on the way and after she took Terri to the hospital and got her some really strong, pain pills, she could yell at Terri until she was blue in the face.

A police car screeched up to the curb and the door opened. It was *not* Angie however, who got out of the dark, official, city vehicle. Terri looked up but the sun was blocking her view and hurting her head and *this person was way too tall. This person* was quite slim and coming swiftly in their general direction. *This person* made Terri wish the ground would open up and swallow her *right then and there!* At least she wasn't barfing anymore, fortunately, because Terri was looking up at the most gorgeous guy she had seen in a month of Sundays. *Hell, a whole year of Sundays!*

Right now, he was smiling at Terri and Gina with beautiful, straight, perfect white teeth. He had wavy, black hair, just long enough under his police cap, which he politely removed when he got to the ladies. He came down to Terri's side, as she half lay, half sat, on the grass. She stared up at him, with her mouth open. He took off his sunglasses and looked into her eyes. *Oh, and his eyes were so brown, almost black and they sparkled and looked at her intently. I must be dreaming, she thought, and oh please, don't let me ever wake-up from this one!*

He gently put two fingers under her chin and with the other hand, he gingerly touched the bump on her forehead. Terri winced but didn't care. *He could just sit there and touch her head and her face, whatever, all day if her wanted to.* She was in foolish awe and the bump on the noggin' was not helping her out at all.

Finally, he opened his beautiful mouth and spoke.

"Hi there, Terri," he said, gently, "it looks like you have quite a bump on your forehead. Do you remember what happened?"

Terri just kept staring at him. *So, he was real. At least he was talking, like he was real and she had to get a hold of herself, right now before things got any worse. Was that even possible, at this point?* With Terri's luck so far, anything was possible.

She asked the first things that came to her mind. "How.... how do you know my name? How did you get here so fast? Where did you come from?" Terri realized, he was the one who was supposed to be asking the questions but she couldn't help herself. She had to be in some kind of shock, too. As always, this was *way too much* for Terri to handle. However, he did proceed to answer all of her questions and very politely, too.

"I work with your friend, Angie." He continued to look intently into her eyes and finished explaining. "I was just down the block when she called and told me you were in trouble and where you were. I'm Officer Rico Mathews, but everybody just calls me Rico. Can you tell me what happened? Can you remember anything?" Terri just shook her head. She didn't want to remember anything. She felt too crappy to think, right now.

"There's an ambulance on the way. Maybe later would be a better time for questions," Rico decided.

Terri looked up at Gina and saw her gapping at Rico, too. *Rico, what a cool name. Spanish for Rick, maybe? Was he Spanish? He was certainly dark enough but come to think of it, Spanish people were not really dark. Italian, maybe?*

All these things were going through Terri's mind and she did not want to think about what had happened, in Ed's house. Oddly, Rico did not ask her why she was near a crime scene. He did not yell at her, the way Angie was sure to. On the contrary, he was being more sweet than any cop she had ever met and speaking of cops, the uniform didn't hurt much, either. What movie was it where the actress says, *"Oh, I just love a man in uniform!"* *Geez, that was hokey. Or even better, "Is that a gun in your pocket…?"*

The ambulance flew up at that moment, suddenly interrupting Terri's silly thoughts. Even worse, Angie in her squad car with her partner, Will, was right behind the emergency vehicle. Angie jumped out of the passenger side, of her squad car and came running up to Terri. She looked at Rico and Gina and without consulting Terri, asked them what they had to say about the situation. Rico calmly told Angie, that Terri needed medical attention, *a.s.a.p.* He also told Gina they would be contacting her, if they had any questions. There was little doubt, that Rico Mathews, was Angie's superior but he was firm, while giving orders and instructions, without seeming to push his weight around.

Angie snapped into cop mode and got out of the way, as the E.M.T.s ran up to Terri and started to prepare to carefully place her on to a stretcher.

"This is ridiculous," Terri said, finally coming to her senses. "I can walk to the car and Angie can take me to a doctor." She tried to stand-up and down she went. Rico's strong arm was under hers, in a shot. *She hadn't gone back down on purpose, honest!* Apparently, the bump was more serious than she realized and finally she agreed to be placed on the stretcher and in to the waiting ambulance.

As they moved her into the back of the ambulance, all she could think about was Rico. *Was he married, engaged, dating anyone at the moment, gay? Anything at all that would keep her from seeing him again on something other than police business, was just too awful to think about. Terri was going to smack Angie, if this guy was available and she hadn't mentioned him sooner.*

The ride to the hospital was of course, bumpy and uncomfortable but mercifully short. Angie was there when they arrived at the emergency room of West Roxbury Medical and to Terri's relief, so was Rico. Now that was a good sign, if ever there was one.

Terri was bound and determined, *concussion or no concussion,* to find out about this guy if it killed her! *O.K., bad analogy but who had time to waste these days? Either you grabbed an opportunity or it slipped away, simple as that.*

After a thorough examination, by the emergency room doctor on duty, it was determined Terri had a mild concussion. Enough to give her one hell of a headache but not enough to keep her in the hospital, over night. She was, indeed, given a prescription for some strong pain pills she was instructed to take very carefully, according to the doctor's orders.

That settled, Angie was advised by Rico to take Terri home where also, according to doctors orders, she was told to rest for at least this evening and the next day. Unfortunately, she had to work at *Twin Pines* the next night but she decided to wait and see how she felt. She hated to call in sick. They needed all the help they could get on Friday nights. Terri decided to think about it in the morning.

Terri felt almost a physical loss, when she and Angie drove away from the hospital, as she looked back and saw Rico standing on the curb, talking with Angie's partner, Will. Terri straightened around and looked forward, as Angie drove in the direction of her apartment.

"Well," Terri figured she may as well begin the conversation, "aren't you going to start giving me hell?"

"You have a concussion, *dope!*" Angie certainly sounded irritated with her friend and rightly so. "I'll yell at you later." Then she really sobered.

"Terri," Angie sounded like she was starting to cry, "you could have been killed. What in the *hell* were you doing in that house? What would I do if something ever happened to you? God, you make me so crazy sometimes, when you do goofy stuff like this. What would I do with those two ditzy cats, if anything ever happened to you?

"Angie," Terri stopped the unceasing queries, "how many questions are you going to ask me today *all in a row*, so I can't answer any of them? I have an idea." Terri was trying to figure out the easiest way to ask Angie about Rico, without sounding too interested. *Angie was so aware of all of her moods, Terri doubted she would be able to get away with anything but why not give it a shot?* Terri went on, with plans for the evening.

"How about, if after I rest for awhile and you're done working, you pack up your P.J.s and toothbrush and come over and stay at my apartment tonight? We'll have a mini-pajama party. You know Louie and Maria just love it when you come over. I've got some great food and wine in the fridge. What do you say?"

Angie looked sideways at Terri. *Shit!*, Terri thought, *she's already on to me.* Terri smiled at her and put her hand to the bandage on her forehead. "I have a concussion, remember? You can keep an eye on me. Also, I can tell you what happened and.......*Oh, my God!*"

Terri suddenly remembered the baseball card. *How could she have forgotten about it? Her attacker had taken the card.* She had seen it laying on the floor and watched, before she blacked out, as he or she, whoever it was, picked up the card. She remembered the person was wearing a thin, black glove. *Gloves, in August?* Obviously, this person was concerned about leaving fingerprints. No danger there, so no point in the police checking for any, if they did choose to search the place again.

"What, what's the matter?" Angie asked, instantly concerned. "Are you feeling sick again? Do you want me to take you back to the hospital?"

Terri caught her breath and tried to figure out how to handle this latest conundrum. *How could she tell anyone about the precious card?* It was gone and it still seemed impossible it even existed in the first place. Once again, she couldn't prove anything because she had nothing solid to show anyone. She told Angie anyway and watched as her friend reacted.

"*Holy shit!*" Angie's eyes bugged out of her head. "Are you sure about this? How is this possible? Was it in good condition?"

"Angie!" Terri jumped in where she could. "You're doing it again. One question at a time. Hello, me, concussion here!"

"Sorry," said Angie, "but do you realize what you are saying here? This is beyond nuts! Those cards don't just pop up out of no where. You're brother Rob, is going to freak!"

At least Angie had stopped asking questions. Terri didn't know where to go with any of the things that had happened to her so far, this day and it wasn't even noon yet.

"Angie," Terri realized suddenly, "can we break for lunch? I haven't had much of anything to eat today. I barfed after I came out of Ed's house from this *stupid* bump on my *stupid* noggin', so can we stop somewhere and get a sandwich? Oh, and I am dying of thirst. God, I can't wait to brush my teeth!"

Angie considered all of this and agreed. It was about 11:45 and she certainly needed to eat lunch herself. "Yes, fine," she said and tried to think of the closest place where they could stop. Then before they had a chance to consider this decision, Angie looked over at Terri, giving her friend, what could be termed as, *the evil eye.*

"What?" Terri looked back at her innocently. *Uh oh,* she could see Angie had figured out something else was up and she wasn't about to back off, even with Terri trying to distract her.

"What happened between you and Rico, back at Ed's house?" Angie asked pointedly, not mincing any words, as usual.

Terri looked at her, amazed at her friends insight. "How did you...what do you mean? Nothing happened. He drove up....," Terri started to stutter, "and he looked at...the bump... on my head and he put his fingers underneath my chin and..... *I thought I was going to die!* O.K., are you happy, now? I'm not exactly the *love at first sight* type, you of all people, know that. We've both always thought that was a bunch of crap, anyway but c'mon, give me a break, will you? O.K. fine, just give me your best shot. Pick on me when I'm down."

Terri was just plain starting to feel sorry for herself and on the verge of tears. *Was it so terrible to want to get to know someone nice?*

"Terri, calm down," Angie looked at her best friend sympathetically, "I'm not going to give you a hard time about Rico but...." she started to explain something and Terri could feel her heart jump with disappointment.

"O.K. so, he's married or whatever, right? I'll get over it, won't be the first time." She felt the lump in her throat getting bigger all the time.

"No," Angie said, cautiously, "he's not married or whatever."

Terri looked at Angie and the silly phrase, *hope springs eternal,* came to her mind. She caught her breath though, as she realized there was something about Rico, that Angie needed to tell her. She didn't think she could be more stunned today. *She was wrong.*

"Rico was engaged." *Was?* Terri waited for her to go on. Angie took a deep breath herself and finished her explanation.

"He *was* engaged, to a really nice girl, we all heard. He was living and working in New York. He was at the World Trade

Center, the day of the terrorist attack, rescuing people out of the rubble. He met this girl because she was there too, helping. She was a nurse and after it was all over, they started dating. They were supposed to get married last year, had a huge wedding planned, according to Will. Will said the only reason he even got the chance to talk to Rico about it, was because they finally stopped after work for a couple of beers and Rico just couldn't keep what had happened, to himself anymore." Angie stopped here and looked at Terri, who hadn't said a word or even made a sound. She went on with the story.

"A couple of weeks before the wedding, Rico's fiancee and her sister, were both killed in a terrible car accident, on the Jersey Turnpike."

Chapter 6

Terri and Angie ended up at Tim's Tavern, on Columbus Avenue. Tim's serves wonderful burgers, salads, anything you could want for a good lunch and the prices are very reasonable. Usually, Terri and Angie enjoyed their lunch at Tim's but today, they were both sad and confused. Terri had cried real tears, after Angie's story. She really was a very practical person, especially when it came to relationships. However, her first reaction to Rico had been real and traumatic and she was sure he had felt something, too. It had seemed magnetic and gentle at the same time, when he had lifted Terri's chin and softly touched her injured forehead.

Now, after what Angie had told her, Terri felt a let-down so strong, it made the pain from the concussion, seem minute, by comparison. Usually, when she and Angie went to lunch and Angie was wearing her police uniform, they had a blast with it. People always made a big deal, when a cop was around, staring and pointing. Terri and Angie had tried everything from acting like Terri was Angie's prisoner, to talking weird so people thought they were on a case.

Today however, was different and they sat in a cloud of silence, both deep in their own thoughts about the problem. Angie had ordered one of Tim's famous burgers and Terri had ordered a salad with grilled chicken. Both girls had to eat and they did, slowly. Terri's stomach was still a little queasy, so she took a long drink of water and another small bite of the delicious salad. Terri knew however, that she would not be able to do justice to her lunch, on this terrible day.

"Terri," Angie finally said something and Terri jumped, startled from her own thoughts. She had to keep from shouting in the crowded room.

"Geez, Angie," Terri put her hand on her chest, like she was having a heart attack. "For crying out loud, do you want to give me cardiac arrest on top of my concussion? *Man, what a horrible day!* I can not even imagine a more bizarre, crummy situation, *like ever!"*

She put her head in her hands and Angie just waited for her to go on. "I *really, really, really* like this guy, Angie. Are you telling me, Rico was *so* burned from this horrible experience, that he has sworn off dating or getting involved with anybody, *ever, ever, ever?"* Terri stopped to take a shaky breath.

"Terri, as usual, calm down. Man, I wish I had a quarter for every time I have said that to you!" Angie was now at the same point of exasperation as Terri and working on the same headache and *she* had to go back to work, after taking Terri back to her apartment.

"Angie, I'm O.K., honestly. I just had to go-off a little bit, to get rid of some of the stress. Actually, it didn't really do me any good, with this stupid bump on my head. I can't wait to get home, take a pain pill, and lay down for a nap, with my cats, *providing...."* with a lot of emphasis on the word, providing, "they have not wrecked havoc, on some part of my place, that I will have to spend at least the better part of an hour, cleaning up and by the way, *it's a nickel."* Terri finally finished her tirade and looked at Angie, trying and failing, to appear settled down.

"Inflation," Angie said simply, actually following Terri's line of thinking, "but by today's rates and how difficult it sometimes is, to actually *accomplish* calming you down, it should be worth at least a buck."

"Has anyone ever complimented you on how extremely good you are at avoiding the issue?" Terri was trying really hard now, to cheer up.

"Not lately but I'll take all the compliments I can get. Listen Terri, I don't have an answer to any of your questions right now but I have to get back to work. First though, I have to get you home, so you can rest. That's it for now."

At this point, having finished about half their food and declining to take the rest with them, they paid their bill and Angie took Terri to her apartment. She helped Terri up the stairs and they greeted the elated Louie and Maria. After fetching a fresh bottle of water for the pain pill, Angie then proceeded to tuck Terri into bed, for the afternoon. *How weird,* thought Terri, who almost never took a nap. *It's still light out. Why am I in bed?* Louie and Maria were a bit confused also but settled in with her, like always.

"Terri," Angie put her hand on her friend's bandaged head and checked Terri's pupils to make sure her condition was still stable. "I'll be back at about 6:30, O.K? By then, you will feel better and we'll make supper and watch a movie, sound alright?" Terri could only nod at Angie a little. She hadn't realized how lousy she really felt or how tired she was. Angie made sure the curtains were shut and the room was nice and cool, so Terri could rest. After carefully closing the door, Angie checked in with her partner, Will, reported Terri's condition and headed back for the precinct.

Terri opened her eyes a little, realized once again where she was and why and then closed her eyes again, to sleep. As she drifted off though, the last face she saw was Rico's and she felt sadness once more, like her life would never be the same again.

Terri woke-up at about 5:30 and was looking into the face of a puzzled Louie. Maria was right behind him and it appeared as if they had been watching her sleep, for some time.

"Honestly, you guys," Terri griped, as she pushed back the covers and looked at the clock, "will you give me a break? Nothing like being spied on in your own bed. God, my head is going to fall off, I am sure of it."

This news did not bother or affect the cats' unmitigated joy at having her home all afternoon. Terri swung her legs out of bed and tested how she felt, standing up carefully, for fear her knees might buckle. Then she remembered Rico's firm hand underneath her arm, and immediately sat back down, right on Maria, which was most unfortunate. Terri let out a shriek and both of the startled felines jumped to floor.

"Oh, for Pete's sake!" She placed her feet carefully back on the floor and tested her weight, on shaky legs. "One thing is for sure about you two, you certainly keep me on my toes, this time *literally*," Terri said, as she got up, more slowly, this time.

She found her slippers and padded carefully out to the living room. Her phone was flashing four messages and Terri was amazed she hadn't heard it ringing. Her cell phone was next to the bed, so if anyone had really wanted to get a hold of her, they would have called that phone. She slowly made her way back into the bedroom, picked up her cell, and saw *three missed calls*.

"*Holy crap!*" Terri was amazed. "I must have been sleeping like a stone!"

None of the calls were from Angie, as obviously, she would have known better. On the other hand, her mom had tried both her cell and her land line.

"Oh, geez," Terri said to the cats, " your Grandma called like five gazillion times. How am I supposed to tell her what happened today? She is going to have a shit fit about this one."

For this, Terri would not blame her mother if she insisted *her daughter* come home, at least for awhile. Terri however, *could not do that*. Not for any extended amount of days, anyway. She had families that depended on her. She hadn't gone on any kind of a vacation, since she had started *Terri's Table*. It was almost scary how fast people became dependent on this kind of a service. They all had young kids and with the busy schedules they had set-up for themselves, sometimes Terri thought these people would starve, if it wasn't for her bringing them most of their meals for the week. The rest of the time, they existed on junk food and frozen dinners. It was pathetic really and Terri was kind of surprised this type of service hadn't taken off more, by now.

"Nobody wants to cook, anymore," Terri said to Louie and Maria, as they planted themselves next to her, when she plopped on to the couch. "Humans are so lazy, do you guys know that?"

Terri tried to pet both of the cats, while she made up her mind what she was going to tell her parents. If she didn't call pretty soon, the phone was going to ring again and she wouldn't have a choice but to spill the beans. Terri looked at the cordless phone in her hand and just as she had her mind made up, it rang.

"*Oh, shit!*" Terri screeched, but as she looked at the caller I.D., she saw it was a *blocked number*. Her heart nearly stopped beating when she realized who it probably was and on the 4th ring, she quickly answered before the stupid machine kicked in.

"Hello," she said breathlessly, trying not to sound ecstatic, "this is Terri."

"Hi Terri." *There was that wonderful, sweet voice again.* "This is Rico Mathews, Officer Mathews, from this morning. I don't know if you remember me but I got your number from Angie. I just wanted to give you a call to see how you are feeling. I hope that's O.K."

After Terri's heart started beating again and she started *breathing again* and vowed in her mind to strangle Angie *again*, for not at least calling her and warning her, she managed to get out a fairly normal reply.

"Of course I remember you, Officer Mathews." There was no way, on this planet, Terri would have forgotten him but she wasn't going to put *that* into casual conversation, anytime soon.

Maybe after they were married for a few years and had two beautiful children but not right now.

"I only had a mild concussion, you know? You were there and Gina and Angie and her partner, Will." Now she was sounding like Dorothy from 'The Wizard of Oz.' *'"You were there and you and you!, she said, pointing at the Scarecrow."'* *Get a hold of yourself, girl, her inner child screamed.*

"Weren't you at the hospital, too? Oh, and I'm fine, by the way. Angie and I went to Tim's for lunch and she brought me back to my apartment and I went to sleep. Pretty boring stuff, for someone who should probably be charged with *breaking and entering* a crime scene." *Shut-up!, she chided herself, before he comes and arrests you. Mmmmm, that wouldn't be such a terrible idea,* but Rico was talking again.

"Um, yeah, we talked about that, Angie, Will and I. Since the door wasn't locked, you really can't be charged with breaking and entering but you were taking a big chance, Terri. You could have ended up with something a lot worse than a mild concussion. You're Angie's close friend and she was pretty shook-up about the whole thing. Oh, and please call me Rico. Everyone does and unless I'm in a professional situation, I have never felt comfortable with the Officer Mathews thing. I hope we can be friends and that's what all my friends call me." He finally stopped talking and there was an uncomfortable silence.

What was happening here? Terri didn't know where to go with this conversation. *Was this just a courtesy call or something? Did he follow-up on all the dopey women out there who got themselves into trouble? How about hookers? Did he call them up to see how they were doing after he had picked them up and hauled them in, just because he was a nice guy? What the hell?*

"Umm, O.K., sure Rico, that would be great. I can use all the friends I can get, especially police officers. You can never have enough police officers for friends, you know?" *O.K., now she was just babbling!*

Terri made a face she was sure was discernable through the telephone line. If she could have lifted up her leg, to kick herself at that moment, she certainly would have. She had fallen down enough for one day however, and she needed to end this call on a positive note. *She just couldn't talk to him anymore, not right now.* Terri had to get her thoughts together and figure out how to break through this guy's issues. She had to find a way to let him know, there *could* be another person in this world for him. He certainly had gone through a terrible ordeal. The terrorist attack, the collapse of the Twin Towers and then the tragic loss of his fiancee. He probably needed more time and Terri was in no rush to get too serious, anyway. So, they would start out by being friends, *friends is good.* She could handle being friends, *for now.*

"Thank-you Rico, so much, for calling," Terri said warmly. "I woke-up just now and Angie is coming over a bit later to stay with me tonight, so I will be fine."

"Yes, she told me, and I think that is a very good idea. Even a mild concussion is nothing to be taken lightly, so having a good friend to look out after you for tonight, is just what you need." Rico sounded as if he needed to hang up too, so resisting the urge to ask him to join the party, Terri said good-bye and shut off the phone. She took a deep breath and tried to think straight but when the stupid phone rang again, she threw the instrument into the air in surprise, spooking the cats and grabbing it before it hit the floor.

"*Damn it!*" Terri protested, feeling her pulse race for the umpteenth time that day and then seeing it was her mom, she quickly answered.

"Terri, oh my God!" Her mother sounded both relieved and upset, at the same time. *Amazing how moms can accomplish that.* "Are you all right? I've called you, like a dozen times today. Your father was getting ready to drive down to Boston to check on you, when we got a hold of Angie and she told us you were O.K. but that was two hours ago. Have you been sleeping? Are you going to tell us what happened?" Emily Springe, finally stopped for a breath.

How many times today, were people going to ask her a series of questions without stopping to get an answer, for any of them? This day just would not stop being annoying!

"Mom, I really am fine and yes, I was sleeping. Then a friend called, so I've been on this line for a few minutes." It was already nice to think of Rico as her friend. *Heaven forbid* though, Terri should even mention Rico to her mother, until she had a ring on her finger, at the very least. If Terri even hinted that she had found a guy, she was the least bit attracted to, especially a guy like Rico, her mother would have a hall rented for the reception. *What law says, you have to be married before you turn 30? Some kind of secret mother's law, in some weird book, written down in ancient hand writing.* Terri was sure of that.

"O.K., so you're fine. Would you or could you, *at least* tell your father and I, what happened to you today? Maybe you should come home for a couple of weeks. You could use the break and it's so much cooler, up here by the ocean, you know that." Emily finished, trying to sound soothing. Terri was ready however, with a comeback.

"Mom, we have talked about this. I have a lot of responsibilities here in Boston. When I can get a little more organized, I will plan a trip up there. But you know what happens when I come home. I can only stay for a few days and then when I have to leave, you get all upset. Where are the rest of my siblings, by the way? Can't one of them just *drop everything* to go home? I'm insanely busy right now, so I can't." Terri knew she was being unfair to her parents but her mom just did that to her. Terri was in no mood for a long, drawn out guilt trip today and now her headache was coming back. *Where had she put those damn pain pills, anyway?* She got up off the couch to go search for them. With the cats running after her, Terri headed for the bedroom, where she had left the prescription bottle on the lamp table.

"Terri," Emily warned her, "you still haven't told me what happened. *Are you going to get on with it, or not?*"

Terri knew she had pushed her mother, a little too far and she did owe them some kind of an explanation. She decided to go for half the truth and hope that her mother bought it.

"O.K., fine. I was at a client's house today. I stumbled and hit my head on a bed-post, that's all. I have a bump on my head but the doctor said I am going to be fine. Angie will be here in a little bit and she is going to stay over night. We are going to eat supper and watch a movie, O.K?" Terri stopped talking and hoped she had sounded convincing. She must have because Emily didn't bug her for anymore details. Either that or she knew Terri wasn't going to tell her anything else and she didn't want to push it.

"Fine," Emily said, a little defensively, "I'm sorry to bother you with my concerns." *Guilt trip, guilt trip!* Terri felt bad then, of course and promised her mother she would call her first thing in the morning, before she hung-up the phone.

Terri looked at the cordless phone on it's stand, charging back up, just daring it to ring and scare the hell out of her again. *Although, if it was Rico, no problem.* It did not ring again however, so she finally walked away from the stupid thing.

'Land lines,' Terri had been considering just getting rid of hers. They were almost obsolete, what with all the cells out there now. On the other hand, Terri was so glad she had talked to Rico on it, she decided maybe she still needed it after all and then went in search of her cell phone. She grabbed it off the night stand and walked back out of the bedroom, to the kitchen, with Louie and Maria at her heels. She got out their food, filled their bowls, rinsed out the two water dishes and filled them with fresh.

After checking the fridge to see what she and Angie could have for supper, Terri came up with chicken breasts, fresh mushrooms, broccoli, and crisp green onions. She looked in the small freezer and found medium shrimp, and took them out to thaw under tepid water. *Stir-fry it would be,* she decided, getting out the ingredients needed for a Teriyaki sauce. She grabbed oil, soy sauce, and vinegar, then searched the fridge again for fragrant, garlic cloves.

The apartment was full of wonderful smells, when Angie knocked and let herself in with her key, to Terri's front door.

"Hey, hey," Angie called a cheerful greeting, "how's the patient doing?" At the sound of Angie's voice, Louie and Maria, who had been taking, yet another nap on the sofa, jumped up and ran to greet the company. Angie got down on the floor and gathered the two fuzz balls into her arms.

"Hi Babies, hi," she cooed to the thrilled felines. Angie loved the cats but had decided not to keep a pet, for the time being. Her life-style just could not handle the responsibility of giving a pet the love and care, that was needed. Terri and Angie actually, sort of shared the cats and this worked out pretty well. If Terri needed to leave them for a day or two, they could either stay with Angie or she could check on them. Maria and Louie were so easy-going, they loved all humans. As long as someone wanted to give them attention, they would take it. Terri could hear them both purring enthusiastically from the kitchen. Angie got up off the floor and came over to see what Terri was up to.

"What ya' building there, girl? It smells wonderful and I am famished! We had something going on every second this afternoon, I swear. Between the domestic disputes and old ladies calling about suspicious characters hanging around their houses...." Angie stopped and looked at Terri, who was giving her an accusing stare. She gave up her cover.

"Yeah, so Rico called, didn't he?" Angie couldn't tell if Terri was glad or not so glad about it.

"Ya' think?" Terri snapped but softened when she saw Angie's face. "I'm not mad, Ang," she said honestly, "it was great to hear his voice but I really would have liked some warning, you know? So, how do you feel about stir-fry? I got chicken, shrimp, mushrooms and veggies, with Teriyaki sauce and wild rice."

"Yeah, I see and it's looks and smells great. I *am* sorry, Terri," Angie went on. "I wanted to let you know but Rico asked me for your number right away and the afternoon was insane. Naturally, no one was going to call you at that point, as we knew you were asleep. You did sleep, right? Oh, and did you talk to your mom?" Angie asked, looking guilty again. "She called me and was she frantic, or what?" Angie tried to grab a piece of chicken, out of the pan, Terri was stirring and got her hand smacked!

"Hey!" Terri scolded, " it's not done yet!" Then she went on. "Oh yeah, I talked to her alright and she started in with the *coming home crap, again*. She just can not get used to the fact, that *I live here now*. I know my dad is fine with it but mom, honestly. I guess it's all about the *empty nest* thing. With Rob living in D.C. and my sisters off at school, I'm the only one she seems to bug about coming home. Not that she wants me to move back in or anything but I can't go home for a whole month, like she would like me to. It always makes me crazy when she starts going off on that. So, *pardon me* if I just don't have time to pack my bags for an extended guilt trip, right now!"

"Are you through?" Angie asked, looking at Terri like she was completely insane. *"Pack your bags for what?* Where did you come up with that one?"

"I just made it up, what do you think?" Terri looked at her wickedly.

Angie thought about it for a second. "Mmmm, it actually fits. What can I do to help, anyway? Want me to start the rice? Wild rice always seems to take forever to cook." She picked up the box and started to examine the instructions on the back.

"I've got a sauce pan right here." Terri said, handing her a small blue pan, with the lid. "Measure in some water and we'll start it to boil. Don't worry, I've got appetizers. I'm hungry too, now that I've started to sort of recover from this weird day. Those pills are great, by the way. Made me sleep like a baby. *Both phones* were going off, as a matter of fact. Mom, natch and I didn't hear either one. So good thing there wasn't a fire or anything. Oh, and have some wine. There's a good bottle of White Zin in there. I wonder if it would be alright for me to have a glass." Terri pondered this, as she finished cooking the meats and veggies.

Angie opened the fridge, and got out a platter of cheese and cold meats, Terri had already prepared. There were also crackers and a couple of wonderful spreads, one being a fabulous *pate'* Terri had gotten from Jack, for a very reasonable price. The *good stuff* was not cheap but worth it. Angie spread some of it on a cracker and made yummy noises. Taking a chilled glass out of the freezer, she poured in some wine and offered it to Terri, before filling one for herself. Terri took it, moved the stir-fry mix of meats, veggies and sauce off to the side and covered it to stay warm, until the rice was done.

"Me thinks you will be fine, my dear," Angie said, as they left the small kitchen. "You are not moving from this apartment, at least not for tonight, anyway and some wine will do you good. Besides, there is no way you can appreciate this wonderful *pate'* unless, you have it with a glass of good wine. Your butcher Jack, is a god. You got a nice set-up there." She moved to the couch with her glass and the cracker basket. Terri joined Angie, with the tray of appetizers and her own glass.

"Well, I spend a lot of money, *there*." Terri said, with great emphasis on the word, *there.* "I don't know what I would do without Jack, that's for sure. Geez, I'd better call him. I can't even remember if I put in an order this week. Oh, and where is my truck, by the way?" This after-thought was not of great concern. Terri knew Angie would not let anything happen to her precious vehicle.

"Well, I hate to tell you this but Rico, with Will following him in the cop car, drove your truck over here and it is parked in front of your apartment, as we speak. *Huh, well I'll be damned, I guess I didn't hate to tell you."* Angie said and pretending to think about it, stopped for Terri's reaction. She got a good one. Terri started choking and sputtering, since she had just taken a drink of wine. Angie started to laugh.

"Ha! Got you back after that pickle thing!" She said, terribly pleased with herself and Terri punched her, with restraint, fortunately for Angie.

"Well, you asked!" Angie fell over on the couch, mindful of her glass of wine and kept laughing.

"Oh my God! Rico actually drove my truck? Can this day get any more bizarre? Can it, I ask you? *Answer me, you little trouble maker!*" Terri was laughing now, too.

"Oh, God," Terri said then and put her hand up to her forehead, *"man this sucks!* I can not even imagine what a *severe* concussion would be like and I hope, I never have a chance to find out. This hurts like hell! *Crap!"* At least she was in a better mood. However, Angie was not done, yet.

"So, Sweetie, not only did your *true love* drive your truck, his gorgeous butt sitting right where you plant yours everyday, he now *knows* where you live! *Ha!* What do you think of that?" Angie took another good drink of wine and dodged a second punch.

"I think you must have been drinking before you came here and *that* is against the rules. *What do you think of that?"* Terri asked, as she bit into a cracker, also covered with the delicious spread. "Wow, this stuff is fantastic!" Terri agreed, chewing.

"I most certainly *was not* drinking before I got here and *you* know it," Angie shot back, "but this day has made me almost as punchy as you, so it's a good thing neither one of us is going, *anywhere.* So, what movie do you want to watch?" Angie had set her glass of wine on the coffee table and was on the floor shuffling through Terri's already sizable collection of DVDs. "How about *National Treasure*?" Angie suggested, as she came across it in the stack she was looking through, "I love this movie!"

"Angie," Terri sobered now, "why did Rico ask you for my number, right away? Does he always do that? I mean, it was pretty weird when he called me. I had absolutely no idea why he was calling. It seemed casual enough and all but do you think maybe he might be interested, *a little,* just maybe?" Terri looked at her friend so hopefully, Angie felt her heart would break.

A lot of women, who had gone through the department in the last few months, since Rico had gotten there, had tried and failed to get him to notice them. He really was a nice person and a very good police officer. He had done a lot of good work at their precinct and they didn't want to lose him.

So, everyone had just backed off and left him to his privacy. Rico was friends with all the people he worked with and no one saw him looking to change that. Angie sighed and tried to figure out what to tell her heart-sick, not to mention concussed, best buddy.

"Terri," Angie started carefully, " I have to be honest. I was not surprised when Rico asked for your phone number. He *really* is one of the nicest guys I have ever met. If he can take a personal interest in someone he has helped on the job, he does. Also, *you are my best friend* and I talk to everyone about you, a lot. You and I have known each other pretty much all our lives and we do lots of stuff together. *Terri and I went to the Sox game. Terri and I saw this or that movie this week-end. Terri and I went shopping.*" Angie would have gone on but Terri finally stopped her.

"Yeah, O.K., I get it. So, you are saying, don't get your hopes up. Can't you also say, *hey, maybe there might be a chance?* C'mon, everybody moves on, eventually. Rico is *not that old.* He can't spend the rest of his life by himself, for crying out loud! How old is he, by the way, do you know?" Terri took another sip of wine and grabbed a piece of cheese.

"Try some of this cheddar, it's great. My cousin, Courtney, sent it to me from *Door County*, in Wisconsin." Terri popped a piece of super sharp cheddar into her mouth and looked at Angie, expectantly.

Angie shook her head in amazement. *"How do you do that? Where in Wisconsin?"*

"Do what?" asked Terri, as she got up to check the rice.

"You go from one subject to the next, without even taking a breath!" Angie tried a piece of the cheese and another sip of wine. "Yeah, you're right, *this is good.*"

"What are you talking about?" Terri laughed. "You just did it yourself. O.K., one thing at a time. Here, I'll show you where *Door County* is." She held up her right hand. "Put up your right hand, like this." Angie looked at Terri, like she had just grown an extra head. "Just do it!"

"Um, O.K., so here's my hand." Angie decided to humor her.

"Your hand is the state of Wisconsin, right?" Terri asked.

"Looks about right, I guess. Last time I looked at a map, Wisconsin may have sort of looked like a hand." Angie still thought Terri was nuts. "So, is there a point here?"

"Yeah, now, look at your thumb. If your hand is the state of Wisconsin, your thumb is *Door County!* Sometimes, it's even called *the thumb* or just *the Door*. On the left side, is Green Bay, as in the Packers, of course and on the right side, is Lake Michigan. My cousin Courtney lives, in Sister Bay, in *Door County*, on the Green Bay side. Her Mom, is my Mom's sister. We used to go there during the summer, all the time and then sometimes, they would come to Maine, don't you remember? You've met Courtney and the rest of my cousins but it has been about 15 years, now. We've all grown-up, so I haven't seen any of them for awhile." Terri finished her geography lesson and went on. "So, now you. How old is Rico, anyway?"

Angie, who was still looking at her hand and thumb went, "Uh?" and then snapped out of it. "Yeah, I remember Courtney and the rest of your cousins. If I recall, she had a couple of rotten little brothers, who used to drive us nuts! Mmmmm, I bet they've grown-up by now, though. Now there's a thought. We should go there sometime."

Angie shrugged her shoulders then and put down her hand. "I think Rico is somewhere in the 35ish range. Also, no, I don't think he should just decide to spend the rest of his life alone but that's up to him. Let's just see how it goes, huh? So, wanna watch a movie, or not?"

After some discussion on which movie, they decided to watch the one that always cheered them up. *Over Board!*, Terri and Angie both said at the same time. It had funny parts that made you laugh and sad parts that made you cry, so it was perfect.

"Hey, have you seen Goldie Hawn lately?" Angie asked, "Man, to look like that when you're 50ish, or is she 60? Wow, she is *still so gorgeous!*"

"Yeah, and Kurt Russell ain't half-bad either, for an old guy," added Terri.

The rice was done, so they went in to the kitchen to fill plates with succulent portions of the wild rice and perfectly done, chicken, shrimp and veggies, with tangy Teriyaki sauce.

"Chop sticks?" Terri offered a pair of beautifully engraved, creamy ivory chop sticks to Angie.

"Don't mind if I do," Angie accepted the lovely utensils, "these are gorgeous! Where did you get them?"

"Internet, where else?" Terri said, flippantly. "Someone was selling them on E-Bay. I don't know if they are authentic but I love them, so let's eat!"

They sat then, to enjoy their dinner, still nibbling on appetizers to go with another glass or two of the delicious wine and watching the sweet movie. Murder and concussions and broken hearts, could be forgotten for a couple of hours of enjoyable entertainment and companionship.

They settled in around 11:30, after talking some more about the strange week. Neither one of them had to get up terribly early but there was plenty to do, come Friday morning. As it turned out, the week-end would hold a few more surprises.

Chapter 7

Terri sniffed the air appreciatively and realized, Louie and Maria were no where to be seen. Usually, they were still at her feet, washing or playing, waiting for her to get up. Now apparently, someone else had their attention, for they had abandoned her. Terri started to get up, felt the throbbing in her head and remembered what had happened yesterday. The bandage on her forehead, was another dead give away, that she needed to take care. At that moment, Angie, followed closely by the cats, appeared at Terri's bedroom door with steaming, hot coffee and freshly squeezed orange juice on a tray.

"Good morning!" Angie seemed to be terribly chipper this morning. "So, how did we sleep last night? Have we had our bowel movement yet, this fine morning?"

At this point, Louie and Maria jumped enthusiastically up on to the bed, taking away the hospital atmosphere, Angie was pretending to create as she and Terri started to laugh hysterically.

"Oh, real funny! I haven't even gotten out of bed yet. I also, seriously doubt these two would be allowed into any hospital," Terri said, referring to the happy cats. Taking the tray and liberally adding cream, with just a smidge of sugar, to the hot coffee, she continued. "I really can not picture you as a nurse. Good thing you chose the police academy instead. Imagine you asking anyone that question and keeping a straight face. Amazing anyone does, as it is."

She gingerly sipped from the steaming mug of dark French Roast and sat back on the pillows that Angie, still playing nurse maid, had plumped up.

"How am I ever going to get out of this bed and get anything done, if you keep waiting on me like this, Ang?" Terri sipped the tangy, refreshing juice and looked at her friend, gratefully. "Who needs a mom when I've got you?" Terri leaned back and then, seeing Angie's face, realized what she had said.

"Hey, Angie, I'm sorry. You know, sometimes stuff just pops out. I know that I should appreciate my mother, more. I really am sorry." She placed her hand on Angie's and squeezed it.

"It's O.K., Terri. I'm never going to stop missing my mom but she drove me crazy when she was bugging me about stuff, just like your mom does. Such is life. It doesn't mean you love them any less but when death comes along, it changes everything." Angie sniffed and shook herself out of it.

"We could talk about this all day but we both have stuff to do. Really, now, how are you feeling? Do you think you should try to work tonight?" Terri looked intently at Angie, saw she was O.K. and handed her the tray.

"Let me see if I can get-up, first. I felt pretty good last night but those pills probably gave me a false sense of security and I can't be taking them all day." Terri decided firmly, as she pushed back the covers and swung her feet off the bed.

"Do you want me to help you?" Angie asked, taking her arm.

"Sure, I guess you better, until I know if I can stand O.K." Angie took her arm as Terri put her feet on the floor, pushed them into her slippers and stood up. She felt pretty good and Angie helped her into the living room and on to the couch. Of course, the cats popped up next to her and Angie went back into the bedroom to get the tray of coffee and juice. Terri picked up her mug again and continued to enjoy the rich brew.

"So, what time do you have to go to work?" Terri asked, as Angie came back out of the kitchen with her own cup of coffee and glass of juice.

"I'm on from 3:00 to 10:00, today. I talked to Will a little bit ago. He's already at the precinct, of course. Geez, sometimes I think all that guy ever does is work! I was surprised when he told me, he and Rico stop for a couple of beers once in awhile. I myself, have never seen either one of them relax." Angie shook her head and sipped her coffee.

"Is Will's divorce final, yet?" asked Terri curiously. "That's gotta be pretty hard on the guy. He probably doesn't want to sit at his apartment all by himself, wondering who his ex-wife is out with, at the moment. Now that sucks, if you ask me!"

"You know, Will's wife was really nice, when you got to know her," Angie said, thoughtfully. "She and Will were just *not* happy. I have never been able to understand why, if two people *are not* happy, why they don't just get it figured out. Stay together or don't stay together, finish it and then move on. Why get into another relationship and just make everything ten times worse? If I ever get married, it better be for good. It is just too damn difficult to get used to someone and then start all over again. I would never ....." but at that point, the phone rang.

"Saved from words of wisdom, by the bell," Angie said, jumping up. Since the land line was the one ringing, she went over to it and before looking at the caller I.D., said, "It's probably your mom." She was wrong. *"Oh, crap!* It's a blocked number," Angie said then, looking at Terri with buggy eyes. "It's got to be Rico! What do you want me to do?"

"What?" Terri put her hands up to her hair, like Rico could see her through the phone. *Why do people do that?* she thought. "Well, for god's sake, answer it and talk to him for a minute. Just let me get my thoughts together or something.... or something....*are you going to answer it, or not?"* Terri started to panic. "He's going to think I'm stupid, or left the apartment or whatever. Just answer it!"

Angie looked at the phone, like it was going to explode and finally pushed the *talk* button.

"Hey, Rico, what's up?" Angie chirped into the mouth piece, just a smidge too loud.

"Oh, yeah, thanks," said Terri, in a stage whisper, "that sounded *really* natural!"

Angie waved her arm wildly at Terri. "Yeah, she's fine, just getting up, I think. We were up kind of late last night, watching a movie. Yeah, I'm on at 3:00. Are you at work already, too? Man, you and Will never stop, do you?"

Terri had to think. *Did Rico even intend to ask to talk to her? What the hell was going on here?* Under normal circumstances, when a man calls a woman's apartment to talk, it would seem he is interested in some kind of a relationship, *eventually*. This *nice guy thing*, on the other hand, was getting on Terri's nerves. She was in no mood to play some kind of a mind reader and since her own head wasn't in that good of shape right now, she didn't have a *freakin'* clue what this character was up to. When you haven't had a lot of experience with *nice guys*, they are just a bit difficult to fathom.

Angie looked at Terri, as she answered what seemed to be a string of questions about work and Terri gave her a piercing stare.

"Does he want to talk to me or not?" Terri mouthed the words. Angie, motioned back, *just a second* and answered a couple more questions about their activities for the day.

"O.K., just let me check." Angie put her hand over the phone and looked at Terri. "Well, pal, do you want to talk to *lover boy* or what?"

"Angie, knock it off!" Terri whispered back. *"Don't call him that!* I hardly even know this guy. Just give me a second." She took a couple of deep breaths.

"She'll be just a couple of seconds, Rico. So any info. come in on who might have been in Ed's house yesterday, when Terri was there? No, huh?" Angie was asking Rico more questions to give Terri time to collect her thoughts but these were things they needed to know, anyway. When Angie handed her the phone, Terri was ready and answered very calmly.

"Good morning, Rico. How nice of you to call!" *Oh, crap!* That sounded awful and Angie making faces in the background didn't help at all. When Rico started talking, however, Terri forgot how dopey she sounded and just listened to his wonderful voice. *This guy should be on the radio!* Terri was thinking, as she tried to pay attention to what Rico was saying.

"I just wanted to check and see how your night was. How are you feeling? Did you sleep well?" Angie's *bowel movement* question, suddenly came to her mind and Terri nearly lost it.

"I'm fine, really," she said quite calmly, "everybody is making *way* too big a deal out of this. Also, I was thinking about what happened. This person who was in the closet, didn't really attack me. I was injured, yes, but only because I was just pushed out of the way. The problem occurred because I fell forward. It's not like they hit me or anything. Who ever it was, I'm sure just found themselves in a desperate situation. They certainly would have had no idea who I was and just wanted to get out of there. Pushing me out of the way, was the only way for that to happen. Maybe they didn't even need to run away. They did take the card though. I keep forgetting that part." Then Terri realized she had slipped. Angie's face took on an, *Oh, my God!*, look. "*No!*, she was saying and shaking her head, *no, no, no!*" But it was too late.

"Um, card, what card? You mean like a playing card, a greeting card? No one mentioned a card in this investigation. *Put Angie on the phone!*" Rico now sounded seriously professional and once again, Terri was on the hot seat. She covered the phone with her hand.

"Oh, my God, oh, my God, Angie! *What the hell have I done?* He wants to talk to you. What are we going to tell him? Think of something, quick, think of something!" Terri was pleading with her friend and they could hear Rico on the other end, demanding to know what was going on.

Angie took the phone and swallowed. "Um, yes, Captain Mathews," she said crisply into the receiver.

"*Captain?*" Terri eyes nearly popped out of her head. *Oh great, just great! They were in deep shit, now!* Obviously, a lie was not a good choice. *A diversion, perhaps?* As Terri was trying to come up with one, there was a loud crash from the bedroom! She started up off the couch, got light headed and fell back down, just now realizing, the cats were not next to her. On the contrary, they both came tearing out of the bedroom, like naughty kids and flew behind the sofa to hide.

"What was that?" Rico asked, on the other end of the phone. "Are you girls all right? Should I send a squad over there?"

"No," Angie said, a little too sharply. "Terri's cats just got into some trouble. Terri needs my help right now, Captain. I'll get back to you, later!" Angie hit *end,* on the phone and said, "I am *so* getting fired for this." She ran into the bedroom as fast as she could and then came right back out.

"It's O.K.," Angie said, to Terri's questioning look, "just that weird picture you had on the wall fell down. I guess the wire on the back came loose or something. Scared the babies, though, huh?" Angie looked behind the couch and Louie and Maria looked up at her with huge, blue eyes, as if to ask, *"Are we in trouble, or what?"*

"C'mon out you guys," Angie tried to soothe them, "it's O.K., not your fault this time."

"Leave them," said Terri, as she sank back into the couch and grabbed her stomach, which had lurched at the sound of the crash. *How good was that timing or what?* "They'll come out in about two minutes, *believe me. Hey,* what do you mean, weird picture? I paid 10 bucks for that at a tag sale," she said, indignantly.

"Yeah, well, unless there's a 10 million dollar Monet behind it, or something, you got ripped off!" Angie said, never hesitating to tell Terri her opinion of her taste and to be fair, Terri usually reciprocated.

"Thanks a lot, pal! Oh man, what was that all about? How did it just happen to fall off the wall, at that particular moment?

Sometimes, I feel like I am living in a sit-com." Terri sat for another minute and Angie waited for her to decide what to do. "What do we have for breakfast?" She finally asked and Angie let out a sigh, with a laugh.

"How about omelets? I see you have eggs, very conducive to omelets, cheese, compliments of the good people of Wisconsin, ham and green peppers." Angie headed to the kitchen and turned to look at her wiped out friend. *Great and it was barely 9:00.* "Oh, and yes, we do live in the middle of a sit-com. Doesn't everybody?" Terri could hear pans rattling as Angie started their breakfast.

"Well, I am going to take a shower," Terri decided, then, "and *no, I do not need any help.* I can manage just fine, thank-you, very much. Also, I want to brush my teeth, about another ten times. I never throw-up but on the rare occasion that I do, I feel horrible for days." Terri, very slowly got up, off the sofa and made her way to the bathroom.

"Sure you don't need any help?" Angie asked, after her, "I can always call Rico, to see if he can come over and give you a sponge...." Terri held up a warning finger.

"*Do not, even go there!*" Terri stopped Angie before she could get out the last word. "O.K., let's make a deal. We know, that I am *very, very* attracted to this guy *but...*" she emphasized the word, "*but* we have no idea what he is feeling, *if anything* and now we have to come up with something to tell him before he fires you and arrests me. *Now stop goofing around and think of something!*" She slammed into the bathroom and left a startled Angie to her pots and pans and the making of their breakfast.

"Well, that's a fine way to say thanks for all my help," Angie yelled at the closed bathroom door.

"*Think of something!*" Terri yelled back, as she turned the shower on. She looked in the mirror and a frightening picture looked back. "*Aaaahh!*" Terri said, startled by her horrible reflection and then, "first things first. This stupid bandage has got to go."

She carefully peeled the white gauze and first aid tape off and examined the bump in the light of day. It wasn't too bad but

Terri knew it would probably go from black and blue, to ugly yellow and green, in a couple of days. She was damn lucky, she didn't have two black eyes. *Doinng!* Right in the head, just like Drew Barrymore, in *Fever Pitch*, a movie she and Angie loved, by the way, as it involved their beloved Red Sox, winning the 2004 World Series. But *that* was a movie. Unfortunately, this was real and it wasn't a baseball. Terri would have been proud of that kind of an injury, considering her obsession with the game. *No, this was just stupid and embarrassing.*

She stripped and stepped under the lovely, hot as she could get it, shower. Even in August, Terri loved a hot shower. She scrubbed her hair, which felt like there was earth and grass in it, from laying on the ground. Then she remembered Rico's fingers under her chin and felt that funny feeling you get in your stomach, when someone touches you or looks at you and the attraction is *unmistakable. She had to snap out of it!* She had phone calls to make, stuff to order for meals next week, lists for shopping at the market, and bills to write out. She also needed to decide if she could go to *Twin Pines* for work or not. Terri was beginning to think, *not*. The pace of the kitchen was just too fast and stressful. The last thing they needed there, was for her to pass out in the middle of the rush. They had enough help to get along without her and if she didn't leave her apartment all day, she had plenty to do.

Angie had the omelets ready, after Terri got out of the shower and had put on a light, summer robe. They ate in companionable silence for a few minutes. Terri complimented Angie on her cooking. The omelets were delicious, with melting mild cheddar, sweet onions and peppers with the smoky, diced ham. With Terri's omelet pan, Angie had formed two picture perfect plates for them to enjoy and start the day right.

After more coffee and juice, with the good food, Angie put their dirty dishes in the dishwasher and headed for the shower, while Terri got dressed for the day. She slipped into pink capris, or what her mom used to call *knee-knockers* and a cute, light blue t-shirt, her dad had bought her that said, KISS THE COOK! on it. When Terri had first seen it, she thought it was one of the silliest things ever. Her father was so tickled however, when she put it on, after which he gave her a big kiss, that she grew to like it and wore it often. Terri vowed to be more grateful, to have such great parents. She could not even imagine how much Angie missed her mom. Terri missed her, too. Even though they both loved Judith, her mother could never be replaced and Terri felt bad for making such a foolish remark this morning. Terri also made up her mind, to be more patient with her mother and more thankful to have her in her life. She needed to go home for a visit soon but her mother would have to meet her half-way. *Oh well!* At the moment, Terri really needed to get ready, get organized and get busy.

She looked in the mirror, as she sat at an old vanity table, that she had picked-up, at yet another yard sale. It was the old-fashioned kind, with a small stool, deep drawers, where Terri stored her hair-dryer, underwear and socks and the drawer in the middle for combs, brushes, make-up, whatever. The top was covered with the stuff she normally used.

Terri carefully put a little make-up over the bump, which was still pretty tender. Then after applying enough foundation, to the rest of her face, to take away the pale look of her skin, and a light blush to her cheeks, Terri used a little mascara, so she didn't look quite so tired. It really wasn't working all that well, though. Terri always looked the way she felt and right now, *she still felt like crap!*

She picked up her cell phone then and called *Twin Pines*. After talking to Judy, who was quite concerned when she heard the story, Terri was told to *take it easy for the rest of the week-end. They were not that booked up,* she informed Terri. Lots of people doing things outside, more than likely. Going to the Sox game, grilling, picnics and such. They would be fine and see her next week.

Terri walked out of the bedroom and sat down at her desk by the computer in the corner where she had an office, of sorts. She brought up her schedule of meals for next week, began to list the supplies she needed to pick-up and figured out an order to call to Jack. She also realized, she would need to get over to Twin Pines anyway, to check her meat supplies and get what she needed for meals, out of the freezer. The meats would then be placed into a refrigerator, to thaw safely, before Monday, when she fixed her dinners. If she couldn't make it over to the restaurant, however, she could call Dustin and he would be happy to do it for her.

Terri then wondered if there was any way, she could possibly get over to Cal's house to talk to Elizabeth. So far, her amateur sleuthing had gotten her nothing but trouble. Surely going over just to see what Cal's daughter had to say, if she would say anything at all, would be safe enough.

Terri was still sitting at her computer, thinking about all of this. Angie was behind her, after having her shower and getting ready to head out. She had errands to run before work. *Was Terri going to be alright? Should she check on her later?*

"You can if you want to," Terri said. "That would be great, as a matter of fact but make it later, for sure. I know, I will probably take another nap this afternoon. Me taking naps, *can you imagine?* I feel like a baby! Oh, and by the way, any ideas on what we are going to say to…what was that you called him last, *lover-boy?* He is going to insist on an answer, no thanks to me," Terri finished and sighed, wondering how she had gotten herself into yet, another weird fix.

Before Angie could come up with any kind of a workable solution, there was a knock on the apartment door. The girls looked at each other, startled and the cats went to the door expectantly, since they loved any company.

"You expecting someone?" Angie asked the obvious question. Terri shook her head and the knock came again, this time a little harder. Angie went to the door and looked through the peep-hole.

"Ah, guess we better come up with something to tell Rico, really fast!" Angie looked at Terri, before she opened the door.

"What?" Terri's heart stopped beating, for like the 100th time that week.

"He's here," Angie said simply.

Chapter 8

Rico accepted a cup of steaming coffee from Angie and took a careful sip. He drank it black, as Terri would have expected and didn't seem in any hurry to leave the comfortable confines of her sofa, at 10:00 in the morning. *Probably didn't have that great of a night's rest either,* thought Terri, her mind already going to places it should *not* be going. Her strong maternal instincts were kicking in too, as usual.

Having children someday would be nice, she had always supposed but in the meantime, Terri tried to look out after everybody else, of any age. That was the reason she had taken the spaghetti over to Ed, in the first place. He had always acted like he was in such bad shape, didn't have food, lonesome, etc. Well, she and apparently a lot of other people had felt sorry for him and it was slowly coming to light, what a jerk the guy had been. There was *definitely* some reason, why someone had decided, whether it was a good or a bad choice, to murder this man, in cold blood. The facts that had already come out about the gambling and drinking, not to mention the smoking, something Terri hated more than most things, were showing Terri, Angie and the police, that this guy had been bad news. Ed had been throwing away money, like there was no tomorrow and apparently, the only person who knew, was Cal.

Rico had already gone over and talked with Cal, at great length. The girls knew some of it but they had no concept, the extent of the money, Ed owed people because of his gambling habit. So, buying cigarettes and booze on top of the gambling, meant he was throwing away a lot of money and pretending to be bad off, to get sympathy from others. He had been fooling and using everyone, who thought they knew him, aside from Cal, who seemed to be his friend to the end, no matter what.

"Very bad people," Rico was now saying, talking about those to whom Ed owed money, "dangerous people. If they killed Ed, the motive could not possibly be more clear. If someone owes them money and that person can't pay, they think nothing of bumping them off and taking what they can." Rico had let Terri and Angie, stew for a few minutes while he casually enjoyed his coffee and they had discussed, pretty much what they already knew.

Finally, Rico took out the inevitable notebook from his shirt pocket, snapped it open, poised a rather expensive looking pen and looked expectantly at the two women. He looked first at Angie, who squirmed uncomfortably and then at Terri, who shrank into the corner of the sofa, as far away from him as she possibly could.

"Hey, what is this anyway?" Terri finally asked, rather defensively, "Some kind of weird intimidation thing or something? You could at least try to be a little less crabby. I mean, you don't seem like the nasty type to me but right now you are giving me the chills. I thought you wanted to be friends."

"I'm not crabby," Rico gave her a small smile. Terri had the feeling she was lucky to get that much. They hadn't exactly been straight with him but under the circumstances, Terri had sort of blocked out the whole thing about the baseball card. *It was just too unbelievable!*

"I'm not at all crabby," Rico repeated, "but you girls need to tell me everything. It doesn't matter how foolish Ed was with his money or what else he may have done to piss someone off enough to kill him. A murder is a murder and if we can come up with any detail, no matter how small, that may help us figure out who did this, we can stop these people from doing this to someone else. People do stupid things everyday but that doesn't change the law. Now, tell me anything you can think of, that could have any kind of bearing on this case, even if you feel it might not be important." Rico finished his little pep-talk and waited expectantly, with his pen and note pad, for the girls to report.

So, they did what he asked. Terri told Rico, who at this point she addressed as *Captain Mathews*, since they were talking on a professional basis, everything she could think of. She started with when she took the food over to Ed and how much she took over, leading her to believe, someone else had been there, having dinner with him. Rico looked at Angie, after Terri stated her theory and Angie shrugged her shoulders.

"So, that's why you were at Ed's house, to see if you could find some evidence to *back up* your theory, is that right?" Rico asked, as he scribbled in his notebook, most likely in some kind of code, only he could decipher.

"Yes, that is exactly it," Terri was relieved he got the point. Before she told him what happened at Ed's house though, Terri first told him about the weird vibes she had gotten from Elizabeth.

"Does that sound strange to you? I mean, I just can't get, the look on her face, out of my mind. There is something going on there and I really thought, maybe I could go over to Cal's house and see if Elizabeth would talk to me. You think I'm nuts, don't you?"

Terri felt let down and deflated when Rico didn't comment on her story, right away. He was taking his time mulling over what she had told him, apparently and then he assured Terri, he most certainly, *did not* think she was nuts.

"Terri, I would never insult you by not taking everything you are telling me, in a complete and totally, serious manner. You have already struck me as the type of person, who not only cares about other people but I also think you have excellent instincts. Just keep on going and then we'll decide where we go from there." Rico said these words, very firmly and sincerely, making her feel better.

Terri went on and told him what she had found and also *not* found, at Ed's house. Terri also told Rico, her second theory, that Ed more than likely, had sold some pieces of furniture for next to nothing, to get money for gambling. Rico nodded his head at this, thinking she was probably right. Terri went on to tell Rico, about how weird it was, that Ed subscribed to the *Beckett Baseball Card* price guide."

"O.K.," Rico said, at this information, "so now we're getting somewhere. The card you were talking about, was a *baseball card?*" Terri nodded and he waited for her to go on. When she didn't, he looked at her patiently and said, "Yeah, so this would be the part where you enlighten me about what a baseball card, could possibly have to do with this murder investigation.

"Um, O.K.," Terri stammered and tried to shrink further into the corner of the sofa. She held a puffy cushion tightly to her queasy stomach.

Terri looked at Angie and her friend nodded. "Terri just tell *Captain* Mathews," she emphasized the *Captain* part, "what you found and what happened to it. He'll believe you, so go ahead."

"Um, O.K.," Terri said, again with a very strong feeling of déjà vu, another weird part of her personality which, apparently went along with her *excellent instincts*. Slowly, she went on, still holding the pillow to her tummy.

"I walked into the bedroom, after I found the magazines and tried to look *for something that seemed out of place.*" At this Rico looked at her, as if she had said something surprising and Terri went on. "I don't remember where I learned that. I just remembered reading somewhere to *check the garbage and look for something out of place.* Well, obviously the garbage hadn't helped me any and you might want to check into how a perfectly clean bag got in there. Anyway, I walked into the bedroom and saw that the bed was the really old kind, with the heavy head and foot boards." At this, Terri touched her fore head and winced.

"Are you alright, Terri? Rico asked then, showing genuine concern. "Are you in pain? Maybe we should stop for a few minutes," *Great, there was that nice guy thing, again,* thought Terri as she kept talking.

"I'm fine but yeah, that headboard was pretty hard when it came in contact with mine. Anyway, I saw an old baseball trophy and it looked strange because there wasn't hardly anything else on the dresser, like it was an after thought, or something. The bottom of it caught my eye because of the size, just big enough to hold a baseball card. My brother Rob collects and sells cards on the internet, so I know something about them. So, I looked under the trophy and the little piece of felt, on the bottom was loose." Terri pictured herself in Ed's bedroom, looking at the bottom of the old trophy and remembered her shock when she saw the card. She felt herself getting dizzy and suddenly realized where this was heading.

"Uh, Angie, could you help me?" Terri gasped for air and Angie was at her side in a split second. "Bathroom, now!" Terri was mortified. *The second contact she had with this terrific guy and she was going to barf, yet again!*

Angie grabbed Terri's arm and got her to the bathroom, leaving a shocked *Captain* Rico Mathews, with his pen and notebook. Maria and Louie had been sitting on the couch very politely but now they ran after the girls and into a closed bathroom door, with a fuzzy thud! Terri was on the floor, on her knees, by the toilet, wasting a wonderful breakfast, as poor Angie watched helplessly.

Back in the living room, Rico sat on the couch, stunned by what had just happened, feeling terrible for this poor girl. *A rather attractive poor girl,* he thought to himself, *when she wasn't getting sick or falling down.* At this point, that was getting to be the highlight of their contact so far. Now though, his radio suddenly squawked at his belt and Rico answered it crisply.

"Mathews!" He spoke into it, instantly irritated. *For cripes sake! They were just getting to the good part of this story!* After hearing a report of a robbery in progress however, Rico hot-footed it out the door, slamming it behind him. *He'd have to explain later and Angie would figure it out, anyway.* Rico jumped into his black squad car, turned on the sirens and flashing lights and raced away from the curb.

Angie heard the door slam and looked cautiously out of the bathroom.

What the hell, where was Rico? She looked down at Louie and Maria, who were terribly disturbed at being shut out, not to mention their sudden contact with a closed door.

"Uh, hey you two. Where did the nice police officer go, huh?" Angie said to the cats, as she went into the kitchen and looked out the window, down at the street. Rico's squad was gone and Angie realized, they had gotten a reprieve. He had been called away and obviously, the situation was serious enough for him to just cut and run.

Back in the bathroom, Terri was sitting on the floor, leaning on the bathtub, which Louie had jumped into. He now had his paws up on the side of the tub and was waiting for Terri's next move. Maria, with the swipe of a single paw, had knocked over the small garbage can and was sorting through it's contents, looking for anything of interest. She found and snagged an empty toilet paper roll and threw it into the air. Louie jumped out of the tub, over Terri's shoulder and they both, enthusiastically chased the piece of cardboard, across the slippery bathroom floor.

"Oh, for God's sake, you two!" Terri was holding on to her stomach, her cheeks flaming with humiliation. "Angie!" She yelled for her friend, whose face instantly appeared at the bathroom door. She looked down at Terri, with genuine sympathy. "Please tell me, that the slamming door means *that he is gone! Please tell me!*" Terri cried desperately.

"He is *definitely* gone," Angie reassured her embarrassed friend. "He must have gotten called out. I looked outside, his squad is gone, *he is gone,* I promise. Now, let's get you up off the floor Sweetie, c'mon."

Terri was sobbing pathetically, by now. "Oh, Ang," she said, sniffling loudly and grabbing a box of tissues. "Oh my God, I barfed in front of him, *again!* This is so terrible and you fixed that great breakfast and everything. *Shit! I want to* die. *I swear, I want to die and I do not want to see him ever again, do you hear me? Not ever again!"* Terri was exhausted and beyond comforting, by this time.

"First of all, you *did not* barf in front of him." Angie tried to make Terri feel a little bit better. "He did not see you barfing, the door was closed."

"Same difference," Terri croaked because now her throat was sore. "Hearing someone barf is almost as bad as seeing it! *Damn it!"* Terri cried as she let Angie take her back to her bedroom, trying to walk, again on wobbly legs.

Angie got her back to bed and helped her change into fresh pajamas.

Terri plopped on to the pillows. Louie and Maria jumped up onto the bed and finally sensing, something was amiss, approached their mistress cautiously. They laid down next to her and were still. They seemed to sense, it was time to behave, as *their* amazing instincts, had kicked in.

Angie brought Terri a cold wash cloth and placed it on her head. She helped her sit up and take a drink of cold water, from a glass filled with ice. Terri fell back down on the pillows and waited to die, like she wanted to, even though Angie had already told her, she wasn't getting off that easy.

After taking another pain pill, that she would hopefully keep down, Terri drifted off into a troubled sleep. Angie took the wash cloth off of Terri's head. She shut the drapes and shooed out the puzzled cats. She quietly closed the door and left her friend to a much needed rest. As soon as she shut the door to Terri's room, the land line rang and Angie picked it up as quickly as she could, so as not to disturb Terri. Although she doubted that anything could, at this point. It was Terri's Mom, so Angie, without saying too much so as not to upset her, told Emily Springe, who she had known pretty much her whole life, that Terri was fine and had gone back to bed for awhile. Emily trusted Angie with Terri's life *and her own,* so she rang off, assured that her daughter was being properly looked after. Angie then dialed the station and talked to Will. Her partner told her to stay put and keep an eye on Terri. After all, she was pretty important to the investigation into the Ed Stone murder case, so staying with her sick friend, should be Angie's first priority, right now. He also, had no doubt, that Rico would agree. If their Captain, had any questions, they would get back to her.

Angie, delighted to have a day to relax, sat down on the couch with Louie and Maria. The cats, of course, seemed satisfied to spend the rest of the morning with Angie, as she turned on the T.V. to watch the end of "The Price Is Right." Good old Bob Barker, what could be more harmless than that? She watched for awhile but just before the *showcase showdown*, she felt herself nodding off. Angie shut the program off and grabbed a throw covered with, *naturally*, pictures of different cats, leaned back on some comfy, sofa pillows and fell fast asleep.

Chapter 9

Terri opened one eye and quickly closed it, when she realized she probably wasn't dead, like she had wanted to be. She was positioned with her arms, crossed over her chest, almost like *she was lying in state. Mmmm, maybe she was dead.* She reached up and touched her cheek and then the bump on her head. Terri opened both eyes and realized the sun was still shining and looking at the clock, saw it read 4:54 and since it was still light out, *in the afternoon.* Then she remembered all the things that had happened in the last two days and pulled the covers over her head. *Crap! How was she going to straighten this mess out? Was there a mess or was it all in her mind? Worse yet, was it all in her stomach? Was she going to be throwing up every time she was around Rico?* To be fair, the first time Terri had thrown up, was on the lawn, outside of Ed's house, so it was before Rico even got there. If she could just get over her, *beyond belief* humiliation, be a grown-up and start over with Rico, maybe there could still be a way to salvage the situation.

Besides, she couldn't lay in bed anymore. There were a lot of things to do. She had screwed up pretty bad in this investigation, so far. Not that she should have been involved in the first place but maybe there was still something she could do and try not to get hurt, anymore. *It was she, after all, who had found the baseball card. Yeah, the one Rico still didn't even know about yet,* thanks to her queasy stomach and the cats, or the weird picture falling off the wall. She saw the picture leaning against the wall, realized Angie was right and wondered if maybe there was a 10 million dollar masterpiece behind it. *How does one look?* Terri wondered, as she pushed back the covers, for like the fourth time that day. She saw the prescription bottle sitting on her lamp table and decided to leave it. The strong pills, were probably what had upset her stomach, when Rico was here. Time to move on and get better, on her own. She seldom took medications because of the side affects. Besides, Terri did not want to think, she was so weak, that being attracted to a very nice man would make her upset to her stomach.

She pushed her feet into her slippers, yet again and padded out to the living room. Terri couldn't believe her eyes, when she saw Angie asleep on the sofa with Louie and Maria.

"Thanks a lot, you guys." She looked at the cats, who were goofing-off at Angie's feet. "I'm the one who is supposed to be laid up, here."

At this point, Angie woke-up and stretched expansively. Terri plopped down, on the end of the sofa and grabbed Maria in a head lock. Her loud purring at the rather rough treatment, never ceased to amaze Terri. She flopped happily onto Terri's lap and soaked up the attention. As Terri stroked Maria's lush, bright white, silky fur and put her slippered feet up on to the coffee table, she looked at Angie expectantly, waiting for an explanation for her presence.

"What are you doing there, Dr Evil?" Angie asked, as she watched Terri pampering the fluffy feline. "Cooking up some extravagant plan for world domination?"

"*What*, may I ask, are you doing on my couch?" Terri asked, ignoring Angie's silly reference to *Austin Powers*. "Aren't you supposed to be at work right now, out there fighting crime or whatever?" Louie finally noticed he was missing out and now joined Maria, on Terri's lap. It was way too warm for all that body heat, so Terri slowly got up off the couch and headed for the kitchen, with her pets at her heels. She opened their food drawer, filled their bowls and rinsed out their water dishes, like usual.

Angie got off the sofa, sat on one of the bar stools by the peninsula counter top and watched Terri dig into the refrigerator for a fresh bottle of water.

"Actually, *I am* working," Angie informed Terri. "I called Will after I tucked you back into bed. He said I should stay here and keep an eye on you. My partner, thinks you may possibly be helpful in solving Ed's murder. That being the case, he advised me to stay here and take care of you."

At this news, Terri's eyes went from still sleepy to huge. Angie saw the excitement on her friend's face and put up a restraining hand. "Stop right there, Terri. That does not mean anyone thinks it's O.K., for you to go snooping around, anymore. One bad experience, should be enough for you to realize that."

Angie's warning, did not deter Terri one bit. "I *do* know a lot about this case," she said, starting to get really excited. "I can contribute something, Angie and I won't get into any more trouble, I promise. The last thing, I want to go through is another day like this one, believe me." She put her hand up to the bump on her head, for emphasis. "So, what do we do first?"

"O.K., hold on, Nancy Drew. Before you put together a picnic lunch and head for the nearest lighthouse with a flashlight, stop and think. I know we loved those books, when we were kids but *you are not* a detective. That was just for pretend. Angela Landsbury *was not* a detective. She just tried to play one on T.V. *I* am not a detective. I've taken a few classes but I do not have the qualifications to investigate a murder. Besides, you are still supposed to be resting anyway, remember?" Angie asked sensibly and Terri couldn't disagree with her, as she felt another headache coming on.

Also, Angie was enjoying the fact, that they both had a Friday night off. Usually, they were both working and Terri was *always* working. Then Angie had another thought. "Oh, hey, do you think you might feel good enough to go to the game tomorrow night? My Uncle Verne, was going to use the tickets but a couple of his buddies backed out, so they're up for grabs. We could ask Amber and Kellie. What do you say?" Angie tried to gage how Terri was feeling and looked at her a little too closely.

Kellie and Amber owned the vitamin and health food store, down the block and were loads of fun. They were cousins and had a pretty good business with their store. They sold soy products, dried fruits, fresh herbs, and wonderful herbal teas, as well as vitamins and other health supplements. Along with some great animal figurines like frogs, tigers, bears, anything cute or exotic, they had a pretty good business. Someone was always in the shop, looking for a gift or the next great health fad.

At the moment though, Angie was still looking at Terri like she was waiting for her to fall over again, or worse.

"Hey, stop looking at me like that!" Terri spotted the inspection, right away. "Actually, *I am* feeling a lot better. You will be happy to know, that *I do not want to die.* You will also be *interested* to know, even after the hissy-fit I threw this morning, that I *do* want to see Rico again. Yes, I would love to go to the game. With this whole week totally shot, ah sorry, bad choice of words there, we may as well get a game in. I also think asking Amber and Kellie, is a terrific idea. We always have a good time with them. I want to get a bag of trail mix anyway, so let's get out of this apartment and zip down there."

"That's pretty much what I was thinking, myself," Angie agreed. She did however, have something else in mind. "I was also thinking, after we get cleaned up and ready for the outside world, that maybe, *just maybe,* we should snag a taxi and go over to check on Cal. It might also be time to have a little chat with the mysterious Elizabeth. You think you might be ready for that?"

"Oh, Angie," Terri was really psyched now, "does this mean you believe me? Do you think the way Elizabeth was acting, might have something to do with Ed's murder? I do, I swear. You heard Rico say he thinks I have good instincts. Well, my instincts were just fine at Ed's funeral and something is up with that woman."

"To answer your question, I'm still not sure but I think Rico might be. I was watching him, while he was questioning you. Now, *he is* a detective and he said, we should consider everything, even if we don't think it's important. Also, the two of us going over there, will make it look like we are just there to visit Cal and we've been wanting to, anyway. Send cops over there and Elizabeth is bound to clam-up!"

Terri walked back into the bedroom to get dressed, *again*. This time she grabbed her jeans and a Red Sox t-shirt. Her other clothes would have to be laundered, of course, after her latest barfing episode. No more of that, she thought and made up her mind to be very careful, what she put in her stomach for the rest of the day. They had to get something for supper, maybe a bowl of soup or something, with some ice-tea. Terri could always have soup, no matter what time of the year it was.

Angie checked in with Will to let him know exactly where they were headed and why. If they needed back-up, which she doubted, Will and Rico should always know, from now on, where they were.

Terri and Angie walked into Kellie and Amber's neat little shop. Terri sniffed the air appreciatively. Herbal tea, of some sort. Even with the heat, *one could always drink tea* and it would be good for her stomach. The four women greeted each other and Kellie and Amber started jumping up and down like kids, when Angie asked if they wanted to go to the game. Terri, amused, watched them and walked over to where the tea was brewing.

"Oh, you guys, tea and biscuits! *Just what I need!* What have you got here?" Terri poured the fragrant brew, into a beautiful china cup.

"That would be, Raspberry Midnight Dreams," Amber informed her, reading off the elaborate box. "Who thinks up these names, anyway? What do you think of it? Now, be honest so we know what to tell our customers."

Terri took a careful sip of the hot drink. "Oh, it's wonderful!" She gushed, munching on a delicate wafer, off a pretty tray next to the teapot. "I will definitely take some. Also, I need a bag of trail mix and do you ladies have any acidophilus? I hear it's good for the stomach."

"Having gas troubles, are we?" asked Amber, the more devilish of the two.

"Amber!" Kellie scolded her. "We don't normally ask our customers such personal questions."

"Actually," said Angie, pretending to be helpful, "she's been barfing a lot, lately. Especially around gorgeous guys!"

"Really?" Kellie asked. They had *her* attention now. "Gorgeous guys, huh? Not sure if we have anything to cure *that problem* but I'll check."

"O.K., so are you guys through?" Terri had stood there, sipping her tea and crunching on another biscuit. "What is this, *junior high?* I have a concussion Angie, remember? Those stupid pain pills that I was taking didn't help much either, I'm sure of that. So, do you have the acidophilus or not?"

"Of course, we do," said Kellie, then getting down to business. "How long do you think you want take it? It is actually good for a lot of things. Look up some stuff on the Web about it, if you get a chance. I think I may even have some brochures here, that list all the ways it can help. It is a very beneficial product."

She went in search of Terri's requests and Amber started asking questions, anyway. They were friends, so Terri didn't mind but she really didn't want to get into any of the Rico stuff, right now. The little bit of time, she and Rico had spent together so far, left even their friendship, in a pretty ambiguous state. She wasn't in any position to even talk about him, not just yet.

"How about we talk tomorrow night?" Terri stopped Amber's questions, for the time being. "Angie and I have to head out somewhere else, so we don't have time to get into the long, weird story right now." Terri went up to the cash register, leaving a disappointed Amber, to wait until the next night to find out what was going on.

The four friends, discussed when they would need to leave, to go out for dinner and still get to the game, with plenty of time. Angie also bought some of the tea and after paying for their purchases and taking them back up to Terri's apartment, they hailed a cab.

Cal's house was a few blocks away on Temple St, so they didn't have far to go. They drove up to the curb in front of the house and saw Elizabeth's Lincoln parked out front.

"We should have called first," Terri said doubtfully, "we're just going to end up making her more pissed off. I know how I feel when someone shows up at my door unannounced."

"Yeah, you barf!" Angie reminded her.

"Will you get off that, already?" Terri could not handle anymore barfing or talking about it for the rest of her life.

"What do you girls want to do, anyway?" asked their curious cabbie. "The meter is running, you know."

"Yeah, yeah," said Angie. They paid him and sent him away. If Elizabeth wouldn't give them a ride back, they could always call another cab.

They walked slowly up to the small ranch, probably built in the late 60's or early 70's. It was still in pretty good shape. Unlike Ed's, that showed the neglect, Cal had taken care of his house. Despite his loneliness after his wife Loretta had died, Cal still took pride in their home.

On the door step, they rang the bell and waited, finally hearing activity, as the door opened. Elizabeth was standing inside the door and Brianna was behind her.

"Oh, my God," said Elizabeth, like they had slapped her in the face. "*What the hell do you two want?*"

Chapter 10

Not a very promising start by any means, thought Terri, reeling from the angry greeting. Angie took over, immediately. They had not either one of them expected this woman to be so hostile, from the start. They needed to be careful or she would call the police. Even though Angie *was* the police, they really were not here on official business. Angie tried to sound soothing and friendly.

"Mrs. Severson," Angie started out respectfully, "we did not mean to intrude. My friend Terri and I, just wondered if we could see Cal, your father. He's our friend and he's suffered a terrible loss this week. Everyone over at Twin Pines is wondering how he's doing, too. Could we possibly see him? We won't stay long."

Terri looked behind Elizabeth at Brianna, hoping the young girl would help break through her Mom's nasty attitude. Brianna, on the other hand, looked embarrassed and uncomfortable. At least she wasn't pissed off at the world, like her Mother. *Usually, it's the other way around,* thought Terri. The kid has the attitude and the parent is embarrassed. Could this get any weirder?

"We met at the funeral for Ed, Mrs. Severson," Terri stepped in, "do you remember? We just want to see how Cal is, really. We are so sorry if we have upset you in any way. We certainly didn't mean to."

Both girls were running out of things to say. Elizabeth did not seem to want to respond to their explanation or their apologies. Finally, she spoke and it didn't get any better. "Were you two girls friends of that *son-of-a-bitch?* Did he spend money on you, *either one of you?*" Elizabeth asked accusingly, making Brianna finally step in, at this point.

"My grandfather is in the backyard, painting some trim on the house, if you ladies want to go back and see him," Brianna offered, politely.

"Brianna!" Elizabeth was ready to explode. "What is wrong with you? Do we really want your grandfather around anyone that had anything to with that man? I'll tell you one thing," she spouted, shaking a finger at Terri and Angie, "that ass-hole got *exactly* what he deserved. If I could have, I would have shot him myself. Mark my words, there were people lining up to kill that jerk!" She finished her angry speech and was grabbed from behind by her daughter.

"Mother!" Brianna spun Elizabeth around, and shook her. "What is wrong with *me? What is wrong with you?* Ed was shot in the back of the head by someone. Are you trying to implicate yourself in his murder? This woman," she said pointing to a stunned Angie, "*is a police officer, so shut-up!* They came here to visit grandpa. Now go into the house and take one of your pills before you have a heart attack, or something!"

Elizabeth suddenly looked frightened and retreated back into the house. Brianna closed the door behind her, joined the girls on the porch and tried to mend some fences.

"I'm sorry about my Mother," Brianna said, linking an arm through Terri's and then, the other through Angie's. She seemed to be very mature for her age and she certainly knew how to handle her mother. Funny how child and adult often times, changed roles. This young lady was on the ball and she politely escorted a surprised Angie and Terri around to the back of the modest, neat house, talking about the weather and how glad Cal would be to see them. Terri looked down at Brianna's long, straight dark-brown hair, with it's silky shimmering highlights. It was the color Terri wished her hair was and the straight, long style, her mother would have killed for, in high school, back in the 70's. She judged the girl to be about, 5 feet, 6 inches, as Brianna fit in between the two older women, height wise, Terri being about 5 feet, 7 inches. She was very pretty and slim, and polite to the extreme, unlike Elizabeth. Brianna chattered on, trying to make up for her mother's bad manners. Unfortunately, as they came around to the back of the house, Elizabeth had beat them to Cal.

"Daddy, please," she was hanging onto her father and pleading like a child, "*do not* talk to these women. He deserved to die, he owed you money and he took the card from you Daddy, all those years ago. It belonged to you and that bastard took it. Do you have any idea how much that card would have been worth? He probably sold it years ago, to some creep, just like he was! Daddy, listen to me!" Elizabeth was beside herself but she had said too much. Cal looked up suddenly and saw the shocked looks on Terri and Angie's faces. Then, so did his distraught daughter.

Cal gently pushed Elizabeth away from him and Brianna ran up to her mother's side. "Go into the house Liz and lie down. Bri," he looked at his granddaughter, "please give your mother an injection, so she can get a good rest, while I talk to my friends, Terri and Angie."

Finally Elizabeth, who had calmed down and was looking very guilty, allowed Brianna to take her into the house. They could still hear her talking to her daughter in hurried, whispers. *She didn't need an injection, she was fine. She wanted to go shopping, and on and on.*

Cal looked up at Angie and Terri, with a welcome but sad face. "Girls," he said, warmly and put his arms out to them, "it is so good to see you." Terri and Angie went up to Cal and both hugged him at the same time.

"Please, allow me to apologize for my daughter's behavior." Cal went into an explanation. "She is not well and she should have never come down for Ed's funeral. As you may have guessed, she did not like Ed. He certainly was not an easy person to get along with, I must admit but she gets a bit carried away sometimes. I hope you don't take it too seriously. It has nothing to with you girls coming here to see me. I am very happy to see both of you, any time."

"We didn't mean to interfere or upset your family, Cal. We are so sorry, Elizabeth is having a hard time." Terri felt close to tears and her stomach was starting to churn again. She looked at Cal and the sadness on his face absolutely broke her heart. *What a terrible week it had been!* Then Cal looked at Terri and *she* saw the *shock on his face.*

"Terri," Cal said with real concern, "what happened to you? There is a bump on your head. Did you have an accident?"

Terri looked at Angie, trying to determine what she should tell the obviously upset, old gentleman. At this point, she was more concerned about his health than her own. Angie shook her head slightly and Terri waited for her friend to take over the conversation.

"Cal," Angie knew she needed to question him. She just didn't know how to, without making things worse. She took a deep breath and decided to cut to the chase. "I think, it is time you told us what the story is, about the card. Did you go to Ed's house to look for this card Elizabeth is so upset about?"

"No, that would be me," said a voice from the back door. They all turned to look and there stood Brianna. "I was the one in Ed's house, when Terri was there. I was the one looking for the card." Before any of them could absorb this revelation, Cal's granddaughter, lifted up her hand and there it was. *The 1952, Topps, Mickey Mantle, rookie baseball card.*

"Where is your mother?" Angie asked suddenly, as Terri and Cal, looked on in shock.

"What, *where is my mother?* Why do you want to know that? She is asleep, of course." Brianna looked confused as she answered Angie's question.

"Terri, you take the baseball card. Could you hand it to her please, Brianna?" Angie waited until Terri had the card in her hand. "Now, Brianna, please show me where you mother is sleeping, could you do that?"

A still puzzled Brianna, nodded and took Angie into the house. Cal and Terri, stood and looked at the baseball card in Terri's hand.

"I can't believe it," Cal said, as he looked at the card. He didn't attempt to take the card from Terri, just looked, she held it up for him to examine. "I haven't seen this card since, well 1952, when it came out, I guess. It seems to be in almost perfect shape, doesn't it?"

"That would be *mint condition*," Terri said, thinking again, what her brother Rob's reaction to this card would be. "When a card is in this perfect of shape, on the baseball card market, it *could* be considered, *mint condition*. Of course, knowing how carefully they grade these things, it probably would not be given a grade of 10. That would be pretty much impossible but a card like this might be worth anywhere from 50 to 70 thousand dollars!" Cal whistled in surprise but Terri's explanation was interrupted, as Brianna and Angie came out of the house.

"Why did you want to see if my mother was sleeping?" Brianna was rather indignantly asking Angie, as they came into the backyard.

"Your mother is extremely unstable at the moment, Brianna. As you were kind enough to show me, she is fast asleep. So, I think we won't have to worry about her, for now. For all we know, in her present emotional state, if she had seen this card, she may have tried to take it and damage it in some way." Angie explained, as she came up to Cal and Terri, to look at the card.

"Elizabeth is definitely sound asleep," Angie told them.

"Passed out is more like it," Brianna said with disgust. "I didn't need to give her an injection, Grandpa. She's totally wiped! She started drinking before I even got up this morning. On top of the drugs she takes, if she even took them today, she's dead to the world. *Sometimes I wish she was dead!*" Brianna wiped away tears now, she was so distraught.

"Brianna," Cal was shocked again, "how can you say that about your mother? She loves you very much, you know that! Imagine how she would feel if she heard you say such a thing!" Brianna looked so sad now, that Terri's heart ached for her.

There were few things more difficult to deal with, than a loved one who was addicted to alcohol or drugs, or both. No matter what you did to help them, it was a losing battle, trying to do it on your own. This girl needed assistance and Terri was already thinking, they should try to help her. Brianna appealed to her grandfather now, obviously fed up with her mother.

"She's so unhappy, Grandpa! I can't even stand to look at her and I can't take care of her, *anymore*. I can't have any friends. I can't make any plans for college. I can't do anything, unless someone else does something about her. She's my mother but it's worse than having a baby and I don't want that either, at least not for a long time." Brianna finally stopped for a breath. Cal put his arm around his granddaughter for comfort. He had not been aware of how serious the situation was with his daughter or perhaps, he just hadn't wanted to face it.

"We will get you in touch with someone who can help you with your mother, Brianna," said Angie, being in the same line of thought as Terri. Then she asked, "How old are you anyway? I can't tell people's ages anymore."

"I am 18," Brianna said proudly. "I just graduated from High School this spring and I want to have a life. If you can help me with my mom, that would be great. My dad is totally impossible, too. He loves my mom but he is too busy and he does not want to deal with her problems. I think he tried years ago and got no where. He just kept sending her to doctors and they would give her more pills and that just made things worse." Brianna was still upset but she looked more hopeful now. Cal tightened his arm around the girl and kissed the top of her head.

"Don't you have an older brother?" Terri asked. "Last I remember you talking about him Cal, you mentioned that he was thinking of joining the Marines. Where is he now?"

Brianna jumped in again to answer Terri's question, on what turned out to be, another touchy subject.

"Yeah he, my brother Brad, joined the Marines alright, to get away from my parents and now he is stationed in Iraq. I am sorry, Grandpa but I don't think that war over there is some great thing. I think it's terrible and I don't want to lose my brother. He's all I have right now and I can barely have contact with him. It totally sucks!"

"I'm sorry too, Bri," Cal said sadly, " I know what it's like to be in the middle of a dangerous war zone. I may be old but I will never forget Korea. As far as your mother goes, I'll help in any way I can. I want your mom to be well again and I want you to have a chance at happiness," he finished, giving his granddaughter another squeeze, making Brianna sigh with relief.

"You certainly are a very mature young woman for your age, Brianna," said Angie then. "Believe me, in my line of work, I've come across a lot of 18 year olds, much older even, who acted like they would never grow-up. So, with what you've been through, you deserve some credit." Angie warmly commended Brianna, at which point the girl beamed under the compliment. "We will help connect you with the right people to assist both you and your mother. It should not be your responsibility, as a normal teenage girl, too deal with this kind of situation, by yourself." Angie took another deep breath and moved on.

"At the moment, we need to figure out where to go from here. We need to get down to the police station, with this baseball card and tell my Captain, who's patience has pretty much been pushed to the limit in the last couple of days, what is going on," Angie pointed out looking at Terri, who quickly made a face at her friend.

"I'm not going to have to go to jail, am I?" Brianna suddenly started to panic. "I did not mean to hurt anybody and I know I shouldn't have grabbed the card but it was what I was there to find. Besides, it rightfully belongs to my grandfather, doesn't it Grandpa?" She looked up at him and he gave her another comforting squeeze.

"No, you won't have to go to jail, Sweet Heart. I'm sure we can get this all straightened out." Cal looked at Angie, then at Terri, who nodded in agreement. "How do I prove the card belongs to me?" Cal then asked the girls. "It was so long ago, when Ed took it away and he had been saying all this time, he couldn't remember where it was. I just figured after awhile, he had sold it, like he sold everything else, just to get his hands on ready cash."

"I can't say for sure what will happen to the card," said Angie, "but I guess, to answer Brianna's question, it's up to Terri, if she wants to press charges or not. I would guess, not?" Angie looked at Terri, who was listening but still looking at the card.

"No Brianna, I will not press charges." Terri looked away from the card, long enough to reassure, the frightened girl. "I said that to Rico, I mean Captain Mathews, right away. I knew, whoever came out of that closet, did not want to hurt me personally. It was pretty obvious too, especially now that I know it was you. You panicked and it was an accident. I'll be just fine, if I can stop throwing up," she said with chagrin and a slight smile. "Besides, if it hadn't been for what happened at Ed's house, I would never have met Rico." Then she stopped, thinking, *did I just say that out loud?*

Seeing the more than interested looks on the faces of Brianna and Cal, Angie jumped in. "Let's not go there for now, O.K. Terri? We need to get down to the police station before I get fired and who knows what else. Eventually Cal, you'll have to tell us the whole story of this precious baseball card." It was still in Terri's hand. "For now, if it's O.K. with you, we'll take the card with us to the station and lock it in a safe where it will be secure, so no one else can get their hands on it."

Suddenly, Angie's cell rang, making them all jump. "*Oh, shit!* Sorry," she quickly apologized, "yeah, it's my Captain." She moved away from the group and answered crisply. "Yes, this is Perry... Hello Captain, yeah...." and Angie walked around the corner of the house, talking on her phone.

"Brianna," Terri had some questions of her own, "why didn't you show your grandfather the card, right away?"

"Isn't that obvious?" Brianna asked, but her face showed enormous relief. "I knew I had hurt you. I really was afraid I would have to go to jail. Also, my mother has gotten so much worse in the last few days. Ever since we got here, she has been more of a basket case then ever. I knew the card was worth something. I'm not stupid about this stuff. I know who Mickey Mantel is, or was. He died, right?" Brianna asked, as an after thought.

"Yeah, he died a few years ago," Terri confirmed. Then she thought for a moment, "as a matter of fact, it will be 10 years ago, on August 13th. Huh, imagine that?"

"How do you remember dates like that?" asked Brianna in surprise. Before Terri could answer however, they all looked over as Angie came around the house, having finished her phone call.

"We need to get to the police station. Cal, it's O.K., for you to stay here with Elizabeth. I don't think she should be left alone, considering how agitated she was before. Brianna, can we use your mother's car? Perhaps, you can drive us, if you have a driver's license. Captain Mathews would like to ask you some questions, too."

"Yes," Brianna said, rather smugly, "of course I have a driver's license and it's not my mother's car. I mean, it was but she lost her license a long time ago. That's what a half-dozen drunk driving tickets and several fender benders, will do to you. *No, it is now my car.*" Brianna watched Angie and Terri absorb this latest information and then said, "So, you guys ready or what? Let's go!"

Chapter 11

On the way to the police station on Centre Street, Angie quick checked in with Will, to tell him they were going to stop and grab sub-sandwiches. This information, of course, prompted an order for food from both Will and Rico, as they had been too busy themselves, to get anything substantial for supper. After figuring out the order and getting together money, Angie ran in and grabbed sandwiches for herself, Will and Rico. She also picked-up salads for Terri and Brianna, along with several bags of chips. They could get sodas or whatever to drink, at the station.

It being a Friday night, the police station was insane, making a previously brave Brianna, feel intimidated and scared. Suddenly, she felt sure she was going to have to go to jail and whispered this to Terri.

"Not if I have anything to say about it," Terri said, putting a protective arm around Brianna's shaking shoulders. The precious *Mantle* rookie card had been tucked safely in to a pocket, in Terri's small hand-bag and she held it tightly to her chest. "It will be fine, Brianna. No one is going to give you a bad time, here. But you need to tell Captain Mathews the truth and we need to help solve this murder case, O.K?" Terri looked at this girl, that she suddenly felt responsible for and Brianna nodded but still looked doubtful and frightened.

Following Angie, they stopped by her desk, in the middle of the melee. Angie grabbed, what looked like a pile of pieces of scrap paper and shuffled through them for her messages. There were also, a stack of papers and files that seemed to be waiting for attention and Angie groaned.

"Yeah, great," Angie griped, "see how glamorous it is to be a cop? Look what happens when I don't come in for one lousy day! It's all this damn paperwork!" She pointed helplessly at the stack.

Then Will came tearing up to them and upon looking at Angie's desk, started to laugh. "Oh, I see you're showing them the exciting world of being an officer of the law. Anyway," he went on quickly, "Rico wants to see you and Terri, Angie. Oh cool, you've got food!"

Angie looked at her partner and shook her head. "Yeah, we've got food and you guys owe me twelve bucks! Brianna," she looked at the terrified young woman, "do you want to sit here at my desk and eat your salad? Will can stay here with you, is that O.K? You can trust him like you trust me. He's my partner." Brianna nodded again and sat in Angie's chair. She smiled as she tested it, spinning around. Will watched her and grinning himself, grabbed a folding chair from nearby. He unwrapped his ham and Swiss sandwich, fielded a bag of sour cream and onion potato chips, tossed at him by Angie and laid out his meal on the desk.

Will was a pleasant guy, with a medium build, thick, straight sandy hair, and sharp, blue eyes that missed nothing. Like his boss, Captain Mathews, Will Collins had been through some intense, emotional pain, in the last year or two but he was the better man for it. At only 25 years of age, Will too, was mature beyond his years. He definitely had no problem spending his supper with the pretty, young *damsel in distress* before him.

"Hi Brianna, nice to meet you," Will said then, putting out his hand. "As you have already been informed, I am, your new friend Angie's partner, Officer William Collins but I would be honored, if you just call me Will." They briefly shook hands. "Would you like a soda or maybe a bottle of water, to go with your salad? I'm buying and there are plenty of selections in one of the machines down the hall."

Brianna asked for a bottle of water and Terri and Angie looked at each other with relief. Brianna was in good hands and appeared calm, for the time being but they had to go in and face Rico now. Terri was not ready for this but *that was tough.* She'd have to talk to him again sometime and at least they were still on a decent, professional standing. He believed she could help and she would try her best. There was no longer anything to hold back. They had found the card, so no one would think it was a product of her imagination. Also their talk, if you wanted to call it that, with Elizabeth had been revealing, to say the least.

"Does *Captain Mathews,*" Terri decided being formal was the best for now, "have an office? Talking in a crowded room like this would make me *really* uncomfortable." She held her bag a little tighter and Angie understood, Terri's extreme anxiety.

"Yeah, his office is down the hall. C'mon, Terri. *It will be fine,*" Angie said, trying to sound confident, as she pulled her friend behind her. "Rico has probably forgotten about you getting sick already. This place is nuts tonight, pretty normal for a Friday. Anyway, he's got so much other stuff on his mind and wait until he sees the card! *He is going to freak out!*"

Terri really didn't feel that much better as they proceeded down the hall to Rico's office. She felt like she was being led to the executioner or worse. *Oh, for heaven's sake, Terri,* she thought to herself, *settle down! He more than likely did have a lot on his mind and solving this case was getting more important than anything, to all of them.*

Carrying the sandwiches, a couple of sodas and bags of chips, Angie knocked cautiously on Rico's door. Terri standing behind her, clutching her small handbag, fresh garden salad and a bottle of water, felt like a dopey sidekick.

"Come!" Rico said sharply and looked up from a desk that, like Angie's, was full of files and paperwork. *Geez,* thought Terri, *no wonder so many cops are grumpy! They can't get anything done!*

Rico, on the other hand did not look the least bit grumpy. He put down his pen and welcomed the girls, with a big smile. "Good afternoon, Ladies!" He greeted Terri and Angie, sounding genuinely glad to see them. "Oh great, food! I'm starving and you've got a soda and chips for me, too. Many thanks! Along with free delivery, I couldn't ask for anything more."

Terri relaxed, almost visibly. Angie, handing over the soda, chips and sandwich, was glad to see her Captain, despite the heavy load and busy place, was in a pretty good mood.

"Sit down and let's see if, on top of trying to get some food in us *and*," looking at Terri, *"keeping it down,* we can sort out some of the weird facts in this murder case, that just won't seem to go away." Rico unwrapped his turkey sandwich, with veggies, provolone cheese and mayo. He dumped the bag of chips next to it, snapped open his soda and dug in. Angie's choice of sandwich was hot chicken breast with tomatoes, lettuce, and mayo.

O.K., obviously, the first order of business, was to eat. Funny how that worked. Without food, no one could get anything done. This was precisely why Terri had made such a successful business, out of the service she provided to her families. Bottom line, everyone always had to refuel, just like filling up a car. *You won't get far, on an empty tank!*

For the next few minutes, they did *refuel* and spoke of mundane things. The girls were going to the Sox game tomorrow night with a couple of friends. *Girlfriends?,* Rico inquired, strangely enough. They told him about Kellie and Amber and their shop. He said he'd have to stop in there sometime, which made Terri feel a bit edgy. She could not imagine the reaction of Kellie and Amber, especially if Rico walked into their shop wearing his policeman's uniform. Once again, *what was it about a man in uniform, anyway? Perhaps, it was time to do an in-depth study on the subject.* Terri had not gotten her soup but her stomach did feel a bit better. She munched on her garden salad and drank her bottled water, while she wondered if she could get a grant for an important study of the *'phenomenon of a man in uniform and the reaction of the American Female.' Mmmm......, she'd have to check in with the University on that one!*

Absorbed, once again, with silly thoughts, Terri nearly hit the ceiling when Captain Mathews spoke.

"Time to get down to business," Rico said, since they had all finished and had covered everything from the weather to the Red Sox. "It's also time for me to see this famous card I have been hearing so much about. Let me just quick go and wash my hands."

Rico went out of his office for a few minutes, leaving Terri and Angie alone. "I can't believe he's in such a good mood!" said Angie, with relief.

"Yeah, well, I can't believe I just ate my salad in front of him and *didn't throw it right back up on his desk!*" Terri said, also very much relieved. "I'm glad we're finally getting down to the gist of all of this, too. If we didn't have this card to show him, I really would not have the slightest idea how to tell him about it. Until Brianna came up with it, I still wasn't even sure if I had seen it. It was like something out of a dream, which obviously, turned into a nightmare. Now here it is and hopefully, we can figure out if it really has anything to do with Ed's murder or not." Angie nodded and the door opened behind them.

Rico came back into his office and sat down across from the girls once more. "O.K.," he said, "drum roll please. Let me see the card!"

Terri slowly opened her bag and took the small piece of cardboard, still encased in plastic, out and put it carefully on to the desk, in front of Rico. He sat and starred at it for several seconds. The fact that, *he did not pick up* the card, made Terri realize, Rico knew exactly what he was looking at. Also, the look on his face, showed what he was feeling. Rico Mathews, was feeling what any man would, who loved the wonderful game of baseball. He was feeling like a little boy, who had found a precious treasure. He looked up at Terri and Angie and almost seemed ready to cry.

Then, Rico got a hold of his emotions. *After everything he had been through, all the sadness and horror he had seen and felt, the Towers falling, the funeral for his beloved Sandra and her sister Cheryl, this was like a ray of hope.* Rico had almost given up hope he could feel good about anything, *ever again* but *this…..this made him feel good.* It even made him feel a little bit happy. He looked up at the girls and smiled big, *really big.*

Terri saw the reaction on Rico's face and didn't know what to say. The fact that she had met this terrific guy, even if they were never any more than friends, was starting to have a huge impact on Terri. Few people would ever have to deal with as much heartache in a whole lifetime, as this man had in a few months. Rico had dedicated his life to helping others by becoming a public servant, an officer of the law. With all he had been through, most normal people might have given up. He had not given up, however. He had gone on with his life and now here he was, in her life. Terri was studying his face so carefully, that she jumped again, when he finally spoke.

"Um," Rico cleared his throat and then went on quickly. "Who does this card belong to? How did it stay preserved like this? *I can't believe it!* I had no idea what it even was, when you girls talked about a baseball card! Who does it belong to? Girls, can you tell me?" Rico was beside himself now with a sense of urgency or panic or something. Terri wasn't sure what emotion he was feeling. Angie spoke first, as Terri was stunned by his questions.

"Captain, Sir, we aren't sure who it belongs to. We only just got our hands on it, before we came back here. Terri had found it in Ed's house and she…." Angie now looked at her mute friend. *"Terri, focus!"* Angie waved her hand in front of Terri's face, forcing her to look away from Rico for two seconds. "Terri, tell Captain Mathews what happened. Remember how you were in the middle of the story back at your apartment and…?"

Suddenly Terri did remember and her face flamed again. "Yes, Angie, thanks for the reminder. I do remember what happened when I was trying to tell Captain Mathews the story."

She put her hot face into her hands and took several deep, deep breaths. Rico immediately got up from his chair and was by Terri's side. She looked up and saw him, as he put his hand on her shoulder and *the ground opening up and swallowing her* scenario, came to her mind once again. Suddenly though, his hand on her shoulder felt comforting and calming. *No, she was not going to freak out and she was not going to throw-up, anymore!* She shook herself mentally and looked up at a face, that was kind and concerned, nothing else. Suddenly, all she wanted right now, was to reassure this nice man. There was that word again, *nice.* Well, that was part of it, wasn't it? It was his genuinely decent personality, which had attracted Terri to him in the first place. She had always felt this way about people. He could have looked like Orlando Bloom or Johnny Depp and if he had been a jerk, that would have been the end of it.

"I'm O.K., honestly," Terri finally said, "no more losing my lunch or breakfast or anything. Time to get down to work. I'm ready to tell the whole story."

"That's good Terri," Rico patted her on the shoulder like a big brother. *Damn it!,* Terri thought as he sat back down in his chair. Terri picked up from where she left off, when she had gotten sick earlier.

She finally felt recovered and rested enough, to finish the story. She told Rico, how when she saw the trophy, the size of the bottom of it, made her turn it upside down and look under the piece of felt. Then she related how someone, Brianna, as it turned out, had come out of hiding and pushed her forward into the bed post.

"I would assume you do not want to press charges, is that correct?" Rico asked Terri, as he wrote down more notes, this time on a yellow, legal size pad in front of him on his desk.

"That is correct, Captain Mathews," Terri said, firmly. "As I told you earlier, I knew whoever was in the closet, had not meant to hurt me. Of course I didn't know who it was, when we first talked about it. Now that I know it was Brianna, all the more reason not to go any further with it. I will be fine and I just hope we can help Brianna, with her mother. I guess that's all I have to report. I had told you the first part of the story before," she left it at that, "and now I guess, we should move on. We need to tell you about Elizabeth and the way she was acting. It was pretty shocking, to say the least."

"Angie told me some of it. Sounds like this woman has some serious problems. I hope we *can* help your young friend Brianna, get some assistance with her mother. No one should have to live like that. Now, Officer Perry," Rico said, looking pointedly at Angie, "if you need to add anything to what you told me on the phone, go ahead."

"I think I covered it, Cap'n," Angie said. "Did you come up with anything on the murder weapon?" Then she looked at Terri and stopped.

"Um, maybe I should go check on Brianna," Terri said wisely, seeing Angie's look of concern. She was not a police officer, after all and they could not let her in on all the particulars of this case.

"I'm sure she's fine for the moment, Terri," Rico assured both her and Angie, "and it's O.K., for me to tell you both. We did not find any information, that would lead us to Brianna or her mother or her grandfather, as far as the murder weapon is concerned. Cal owns a hunting rifle but I'm sure that he hasn't used it for some time and since that type of gun was not used in the shooting of Ed Stone, then obviously, we are still looking for the gun that was involved." But he still had the card on his mind.

"O.K., so back to this card in front of me." Rico was starring at it again, with the same look as before. Terri certainly knew how he felt.

"You more then likely will have to talk to Cal Johnson about the card," said Terri. "It would seem, actual ownership of it, is a matter of some confusion. It would also seem, Cal is supposed to own the card but I'm not sure if he is going to be able to prove it, with Ed gone." She looked at Angie and saw that her friend agreed.

"That is an interesting point," said Angie. "At first, I have to admit, it did occur to me, that Cal may have killed Ed when

I found out about the card. On the other hand, if Cal had committed the murder, the card may have never been found." Terri looked at Angie, appalled by her words.

"Angie, how could you have ever thought Cal could possibly kill Ed? They were best friends for like, ever! Cal is one of the sweetest guys I have ever known in my life. He has been devastated by Ed's death!" Terri thought she couldn't be shocked anymore, before Angie's words.

"Terri," Rico looked at her sympathetically, "you have to understand. There are all kinds of reasons, for people to take the life of another human being. No one is accusing your friend Cal of anything but we have to look at all the angles. Certainly, by the way his daughter Elizabeth was acting," he said, looking over his notes, " she had a possible motive. Not only is this woman extremely unstable, but she was heard by both of you, saying she hated Ed Stone, although we don't know why. She mentioned the card to her father, said she had wanted to kill Ed, herself. Quite often, when someone is in that kind of a state, they just come right out and make a confession, as it were." Rico then looked at Angie. "Have we checked into the whereabouts of Elizabeth Severson on the night of the murder?" He looked at his notes again and Angie shrugged, not sure.

"We could ask Brianna," Terri put in cautiously, "she is so angry with her mother right now, I think one way or another, she would tell you the truth. I also can't see Brianna covering for Elizabeth, if she thinks that she might be involved in Ed's death. Although, like you said," Terri was still looking at Rico, "people do extreme things for a lot of strange reasons. I guess I can't see Brianna wanting her mother to go to jail, either. *I don't know, anymore.*" Terri put her hand up to her forehead for the zillionth time that day and felt the still, very sore bump. *She so could have done without this concussion! She hoped it would not have any lasting repercussions, on her already mixed up mind. She had enough trouble keeping her wits about her, the way it was.*

"I think I *should* talk to Brianna. She might possibly be able to shed some light on the ownership of this baseball card," said

Rico, who still could not take his eyes off the card. "Oh and Terri," Rico looked at her and seemed puzzled, "how did you know what this card was, when you found it? It isn't exactly a subject a lot of people know about, collecting sports cards, I mean."

"Yes," Terri said, a little defensively, "I know what you mean and I knew right away, what it was. My brother Rob collects sports cards, has for as long as I can remember. He buys and trades cards on the Web. We always joked about this card but the idea of one being out there well, it just didn't seem possible. But there it is, as you can see. How it ended up still in this good of shape after all this time, your guess is as good as mine." Terri finished and felt like she was ready for another nap. *She certainly wouldn't have time for a day like this one again, any time soon!*

Rico however, did have a theory about the card. "Sometimes," he said thoughtfully, "the card has been found in unlikely places, where it may have been for years. Maybe an old program from the ball park or an old book or photo album. Ed must have found it some time ago but not so long, that when he did come across it, he took care of it. If Ed ever did intend to give it back to Cal, providing he took it from him in the first place, he figured out it was worth quite a lot of money and obviously changed his mind. He then, must have hid it under the trophy for safe keeping and probably would have sold it, to start paying his debts. He might have even told someone to whom he owed money, about the card and they may have killed him, when he wouldn't give it up. Mmmmm, now there's a theory we haven't thought of before." Rico sat back and looked at the girls for an opinion.

"We didn't think of it before, Cap'n," Angie put in, "because we didn't have the card until now. It does shed a whole new light on this weird investigation, though."

"Yeah it does, doesn't it?" Rico touched the corner of the card now and made a decision. "If it's O.K. with you girls, I think that this card should be put into a safe, for now. It could be worth as much as 70 thousand dollars! It really should be in a museum, I think. As much as I would like to own it myself, it would be selfish not to share it with the rest of the world."

At this point, after getting no reason from the girls not to, Rico carefully picked up the card, walked over to a small safe on a shelf in his office, opened it and placed the card safely inside. After shutting the door of the safe and turning the knob, he sat back down. "I guess I'd better talk to Brianna, now. Terri, could you go and get her please."

Just then, Rico's phone rang and after answering it, the look on his face became serious. He talked for a couple of minutes in terse, short sentences. He then put the phone down and picked up his cap. "Unfortunately, you ladies will have to excuse me, as I have been called away on urgent business. Thank-you, Terri and would you please make my apologies to Brianna and see if she can come back in the morning? Officer Perry, I will see you later."

Terri and Angie got up and looked at each other in confusion, as Rico escorted them out of his office. After shutting and locking the door, he hurried away. As Terri watched Rico walking quickly down the hall, she again felt that strong sense of loss. She forced herself to shake it off however and looked at Angie for answers.

"What *the hell* was that all about?" Terri asked Angie impatiently, suddenly finding herself rather annoyed. She plunked down on to a random chair sitting in the hall, next to Rico's office door. "Does he do that often?"

"I wouldn't say often," Angie carefully chose her words, "but it has happened before. I think, it's a family emergency or something. That's another thing Terri. There's still an awful lot we don't know about Rico. He's a very private person. That's one of the reasons he never dated anybody around here, at least that I know of. He just keeps to himself so much and I guess he's not ready to let anybody else in, yet." Angie looked sympathetically at Terri, who was once again exhausted and confused.

"Hey Terri, you O.K?" Angie asked, putting a hand on her shoulder. She was alarmed then, to feel Terri shaking.

"No, I am not O.K.! Not even the least bit, am I O.K. I feel like shit!" Terri answered, drained and defeated. She knew they would have to go around the corner and tell Brianna….. *what?, nothing?* She had come down here, driven them down here, as a matter of fact, expecting to get somewhere with this mess. She was also expecting their help. *How could they let this vulnerable young woman, go back to her unstable mother?* Angie was thinking along the same lines as Terri.

"Do you want me to call Cal and see how Elizabeth is doing, while you go talk to Brianna? Can you stand and walk?" Angie searched Terri's face for answers. For once, they were both stumped. Terri stood up on legs, that felt like rubber. Then she got a hold of herself.

"Yes, I can walk, thanks," Terri said, firmly. "I will go talk to Brianna while you call Cal and then we'll go from there." Angie agreed and went off to call Cal, somewhere away from her desk, so Brianna couldn't hear. Terri walked the other way, towards Will and the still, frightened young girl.

"Hi, Brianna," Terri said, trying to sound cheerful. "Hey Will, thanks for looking after our young friend, here." Terri put her hand on Brianna's shoulder, as she was still sitting in Angie's chair. They had finished their supper and Brianna was looking at a fashion magazine, Will had dug up somewhere. Terri noticed it was from last year, in October which was pretty typical. *Did anyone have up-to-date magazines in public places, besides libraries? Another chance for an in-depth study, perhaps?*

Brianna saw, right away, that something was up. "What's going on," she asked, starting to panic again, "am I going to be questioned or not?"

Terri took another deep breath. "Um, not," she said and saw the relief on Brianna's face. "Captain Mathews was called away, family emergency or something." Terri noticed an understanding expression on Will's face, right away. *So, this was a regular occurrence with Rico. Interesting and of course, puzzling at the same time. Oh well, another day perhaps.* Terri certainly had more time than anything else and other things to worry about.

Right now, her first priority was Brianna. Terri could not stand the thought of taking her back to her mother and there was Cal to consider. He certainly could not handle Elizabeth on his own. Obviously, that was something his granddaughter had been doing for some time and it was taking it's toll on Brianna. The problem was solved sooner than Terri would have thought. She heard Angie and looked up, to see her walking towards them. Brianna and Terri, looked at Angie expectantly.

"I have some good news, well sort of." Angie cleared her throat and went on. "Shortly after we left Brianna, your Mom woke up and became very upset when she realized you were gone."

Brianna jumped up, out of Angie's chair, instantly agitated and grabbed her purse. "I need to get back there to her, she needs me!" Her voice took on a sense of urgency as she started towards the door but Angie stopped her.

"Brianna, wait!" Angie put her hand on the girl's arm to keep her from taking off. "Your mother is not there anymore. Your grandfather called your father. Cal had already called an ambulance and your mother is on her way to a hospital right now. It seems that your father, did not realize how bad the situation was. You and your mother were covering it up and your dad was too busy to see through it. Why didn't you tell him what was going on?" Angie gave Brianna a kind look and searched her face for answers.

They all looked at Brianna and saw the shock, on her face. Suddenly, she fell back into Angie's chair and could no longer control her emotions. She dropped her bag, put her head down on the desk and began to sob, uncontrollably.

Chapter 12

By the time Terri and Angie got Brianna calmed down, with the helpless Will standing by, it was nearly 8:00. With Angie driving the plush, new Lincoln Continental and Terri talking quietly with Brianna, they headed back to Cal's house to pick up some of her things. Brianna had spoken to her father and her grandfather, on her cell and it had been decided she would stay with Terri, for the night. Her father, David Severson, would drive down the next day and pick up his daughter. He was renting a car, so they would drive the Lincoln back to New York. The man was finally taking the time to look after his family and Terri hoped it wasn't too late.

Driving the gorgeous, expensive new car, Angie commented on the luxury. "It certainly has all the bells and whistles," she said appreciatively, trying the radio and checking all the gadgets on the dash. "I hope you can take care of this car, Brianna. It's a beaut!" Angie maneuvered the car carefully around corners and up to traffic lights. "I can't even own *a car*, much less one like this." Then seeing Brianna's face, she apologized for seeming flip. "Sorry, Brianna, that sounded really stupid. I should think before I open my big mouth, sometimes."

"Oh, that's O.K., Angie," Brianna said, not the least bit offended, "don't worry about it. Actually, Daddy owns it but the car is in my name, now. My mom really didn't drive this one much. She wrecked a lot of other cars, nice ones, too. She always found a way to make it look like someone else's fault and Daddy's money always got her out of it."

Brianna sighed heavily and went on but she spoke bitterly, now. "Yeah, having money is nice, sometimes," she thought for a second, "but none of us have ever been happy, so what's the difference? When I was in grade school and even up into Junior High, the friends I had, the ones I liked the most, were the ones my mother didn't want me to hang with. They didn't have money so they weren't good enough, I guess. What the hell good has this stupid money done us, anyway? It won't bring my brother Brad back anytime soon. He didn't even have to go. He went because he didn't want to be around our mother. It just plain sucks!"

Terri couldn't do anything about Brianna's brother but she could do something else. "You know Brianna, I think maybe, it might be a good idea for you to look up some of your friends, the ones you liked, for starts. You might be pleasantly surprised. I can't believe how much my classmates changed, after we got out of school. Remember when we went to our 10 year class reunion, Angie? Everybody had a great time and no one thought about who hung out with who. We all talked to everyone at the reunion and all that High School garbage, was forgotten. When you get out into the real world, it's not like school anymore. You've gone through all of that adolescent crap and you can move on past old grudges and the crummy memories. I'll admit, there are some people who never grow-up, Angie told you that, already. She sees it in her line of work everyday. Most people do grow-up, however and I think you would be surprised, if you try to contact some old pals. Just explain the situation, ask them out for coffee or something and you'll find out they have problems, too. Most people just want to talk and have someone to lean on." Terri watched Brianna's face and wondered if she had gotten through to her.

Angie finally jumped in then. "Hey Terri, who gave you a license to practice psychiatry?" That made Brianna laugh, as they pulled up to the house. "Besides, we're here. Look, there's Cal, waiting for us."

Brianna jumped out of the car and ran up to her grandfather, who greeted her with open arms. They hugged ferociously and Cal kissed the top of Brianna's silky, brown hair. Angie and Terri watched them from the car, letting them have their privacy. When Brianna went into the house to get her things, they got out and walked over to Cal.

He looked very grim, as the girls came up to him. "Thank-you Terri, for having Brianna, for tonight. She seems to really like and trust you girls. It will be nice for her, to be some where she can just relax for awhile." Cal looked so sad, that Terri reached out and put her hand on his arm.

"Cal, are you going to be O.K? Do you have any friends you can call, someone to talk to, maybe go have a couple of beers with or something?" Terri was worried about her old friend. However, Cal had another matter on his mind, he needed to discuss with Angie and Terri first.

"I need to tell you girls something, before Brianna comes back out of the house." Angie and Terri waited and knew instinctively it was bad. "When I found Elizabeth earlier, she had taken a whole bottle of narcotics. She tried to kill herself. I lied to Brianna and to you Angie, when you called and I'm sorry. I couldn't wake Elizabeth up and so I called an ambulance and David. The E.M.T.s, managed to get her conscious but just barely. She's still here in Boston, in a hospital. When David gets here tomorrow, he'll tell Brianna. For tonight, could you just take care of her please? I'll be fine." Cal finished his story, looking to the girls for understanding.

Terri and Angie, though shocked again, for the umpteenth time that day, agreed to be discreet. Terri looked up as Brianna came out of the house. She looked genuinely excited about spending some time with the two women and when Cal saw her, he relaxed a little. Brianna had the same concern for her grandfather, as Terri and Angie.

"Are you going to be O.K., Grandpa?" She looked at him, as he put his arm around her, again. "I don't want to leave you alone." She hugged him convulsively. It was clear to see the close relationship between the young girl and her grandfather and Terri envied her, a little. She had lost all her grandparents a long time ago but she had a good relationship with both of her parents, even with the guilt trips and she felt grateful for that. Maybe someday, if Elizabeth could be rehabilitated, she and her daughter could salvage their relationship. It would be a long time coming, though.

Cal, in the meantime, reassured Brianna he would be fine. He was going to the local neighborhood hang-out with some of his Army buddies, to have supper and probably play gin, so he wouldn't be alone all evening.

Terri sighed with relief and exhaustion but for once, Angie did not ask her if she was alright. She knew she needed to get her friend home.

"Let's get you two back to Terri's apartment. Time to end this terrible day. Hey, Brianna," Angie asked then, as an after-thought, "do you like cats?"

"Cats?" Brianna looked confused at the question. "Uh, of course, what…why do you ask?"

When Terri opened the door to her apartment, Louie and Maria raced up. Brianna let out a cry of surprise and dropping her over-night bag, fell to her knees to embrace the equally excited pair.

"Oh, Terri," she said, delighted, "they are so gorgeous! I always wanted a cat and was never allowed one. Oh, you guys are so sweet, *yes you are.*" She fussed over the two, like they were the most precious things in the world and Louie and Maria of course, took full advantage of the situation. Terri and Angie watched amused, as Brianna left her bags and went over to plop on the couch, with the two thrilled fuzz-balls. They could hear the cats enthusiastically purring, as they watched by the door.

"I am going back to my apartment and sleep like a log," said Angie, hugging Terri. "I'll call you tomorrow. You going to be O.K. for going to the game?"

"Absolutely," said Terri, without a doubt. "After today, it will be so nice to just relax and have a good time. Even if they don't win but I predict they will, it will still be a good time. Oh and hey, where do you want to go for dinner? I had better call and make some reservations."

They decided on *Al Dente Ristorante*, for dinner and Terri got on the phone immediately. She made reservations for 5:00, for the four women. *Al Dente* had wonderful Italian food and of course, fabulous drinks, although Terri doubted she would be doing much drinking. Also, the restaurant was only about fifteen minutes from Fenway and the staff would call a taxi for them, when they were done with dinner.

Angie left, to walk the three blocks to her apartment and crash for the night. Terri then called *Twin Pines* and told Dustin, who was glad to help, what meats to get out of her section of the freezer. By Monday morning, when she got to the restaurant to make her meals, the meats would be safely thawed in the big walk-in refrigerator.

Brianna had made herself at home, picking up the remote and turning on the T.V., while Louie and Maria scrambled all over each other, trying to get her attention. Terri literally *fell* down on to the comfy cushions, which prompted Louie, who had been on top of the sofa, to jump on top of her head.

"Ow!" Terri flinched and grabbed the excited cat, by the scruff. She looked right into his face and scolded him. "Do you mind? I'm injured here!" Terri tried to sound fierce but *no*, Louie didn't mind one bit and he struggled to get out of her grasp. Brianna laughed and grabbed him and Terri laughed, too. She laughed a little too much, as it was and Terri started to wonder, if maybe she wasn't getting a bit hysterical.

"Brianna, if it's O.K. with you, I am going to bed," she said with a heavy sigh. "I am, frankly, more tired than I have ever been in my whole life. Get whatever you want or can find in the fridge to eat and drink, except alcohol, that is. I wouldn't want to be accused of serving a minor," Terri said firmly.

"You don't have to worry about me, Terri," Brianna assured her. "I do not drink and I don't think you need to wonder why. You get yourself to bed. I am going to play with these two and watch *'The Tonight Show.'* I hardly ever get to watch T.V., 'cause my mom always seems to need me for something. It's O.K., I'll be fine, now that I know she is getting some help. You have no idea how relieved I am and I just love these two, yes I do," she gushed, hugging the ecstatic cats. "You get some rest." Then looking at the bump on Terri's head, her face turned sober. "God Terri, I am so sorry again about what happened. Are you sure you're going to be alright? I've never injured anyone in my life and it just makes me feel horrible even thinking about it." She scratched Maria under the chin and watched Terri's face, looking for reassurance, that all was well.

"It's O.K., Brianna. Granted, getting a bump on the noggin' would never be my first choice but it's already been a catalyst for a lot of important things getting done. Your mom is getting help. We have the baseball card." Brianna looked at Terri a little doubtfully, as she went on. "One way or another, we have the card. I was actually starting to think, it was a figment of my imagination. Then you came forward with it, that's the important thing. Now, before I fall asleep right here, let me show you where you can crash for the night, whenever you're ready."

Terri showed Brianna the guest bedroom, which is a wonderful luxury when you have a small apartment. She also directed her to the bathroom and kitchen and told her to dig in the fridge, as she had said before.

Terri went into the bathroom then, washed her face and looked in the mirror. She had never seen her reflection quite so wane. The bump was starting to turn nasty colors and her eyes were watery and red. *Shit!, what a crappy day,* she thought. *Actually, two crappy days!* A lot had been accomplished though, awful as it had been. As she had reassured her new young friend, they had found the card, found out Brianna had been in the house and of course had taken the card. They had gotten Elizabeth started on the path, hopefully to recovery. They were helping Brianna get her life together. All of this but *they were still no closer to knowing who had murdered Ed.*

When Terri finally climbed into bed, her last thought was the gun. *Gun, gun, who's got the gun?* She felt like she was in the middle of a complicated episode of 'Nero Wolfe' or 'Ellery Queen.' "*Hold on there, Nancy Drew,*" Terri imagined Angie saying, as she fell into a troubled but sound sleep, "*and don't ever go down into the basement without a flashlight!*"

Chapter 13

For the second time, in as many days, Terri woke up to the smell of fresh coffee and someone else, besides herself, making breakfast. She sat up and realized, she finally felt better. Looking at the clock, she saw it was nearly 9:00, so she had slept for almost 12 hours. That being the case, she hopped up and ran, past a surprised Brianna, who was at the stove, into the bathroom.

The necessities taken care of, Terri threw some water on her face and looking once again, in the mirror, saw a better face staring back. *Whew!*

Still a bump on the head of course but not as tired. Her stomach felt better, so she went out into the kitchen, to see what was cooking, literally. To Terri's surprise, Brianna was making pancakes. A plate of crisp bacon was next to the stove and covered with a clear lid, to keep warm.

"Mmmm," Terri picked up the lid and scooped up a piece of bacon to munch on, while she went to the cupboard, for her favorite coffee mug. "Brianna, this is wonderful," she said, appreciatively. "I didn't think most people your age did a lot of cooking but I guess that's what I get for stereo-typing." She added cream and her little bit of sugar, to the coffee and took an aromatic sip. It was wonderful, judging by the look on Terri's face. Brianna watched her, satisfied she was giving something back, for what Terri had done for her.

"That's O.K., you are right, though. I mean about a lot of kids my age, not knowing how to cook. It's just too easy to let other people feed you, fast food garbage, or whatever. We always had a cook, when I was growing up. That's the *having money* thing again, but in this case, we also had a great housekeeper. She was more of a mom to me than my actual mother and our cook, Louise, was great too. Daddy always hired the best people. Anyway, Annette, our housekeeper, who still helps as much as she can, got me and Brad into the kitchen and made sure Louise taught us the basics. I love to cook, anyway. It's not just fun, it's satisfying." Brianna looked at Terri and grinned. "Ah, I would imagine you already know that." Terri grinned back, in spite of herself, at that remark.

"Oh yeah, cooking is *very* satisfying and I make a pretty good living at it, too," Terri said and then, thought for a second, as she watched Brianna expertly prepare their breakfast. She flipped out four perfectly prepared silver dollar pancakes onto a waiting plate. Brianna even had syrup, warming in a pan of water. As Terri went into her room and got dressed, Brianna made the rest of the pancakes. Terri was overwhelmed and impressed, as they sat down to a perfectly set table, with napkins, silver ware and glasses, of yes, again, freshly squeezed orange juice.

"I see you also know how to set a table," Terri remarked, noting that Brianna knew where to put eating utensils, what piece on which side of the plate and so on. She had also managed to find cloth napkins and some of Terri's pretty napkin rings, setting them neatly next to their plates.

The pancakes were delicious, fresh buttermilk, not made from a mix. Along with the crisp bacon and warm syrup, Terri felt spoiled. "Oh, Brianna, this is wonderful. You are an amazing young woman!" Terri complimented her and Brianna glowed under the praise.

An idea was forming in Terri's mind and it was a good one. She realized, then, that the concussion hadn't hurt her one bit. As a matter of fact, it may be the best concussion she would ever have and hopefully *the only one*, she thought grimly. She had also noticed Brianna's perfect motions, as she ate, the way she handled her knife and fork. Her table manners, like her cooking, were impeccable. All of these things left no doubt, as to what Terri wanted to do. She put down her knife and fork, delicately wiped her mouth and laid her napkin to the side of her plate. Brianna then saw the look on Terri's face.

"What is it?" she asked, looking concerned. "Is something wrong?"

"No, Brianna," Terri smiled warmly at the girl, "quite the opposite. Everything is right, in every way. The breakfast, the table and your perfect manners. You're education thus far, has served you well. If I had been giving you a test, you would have passed with flying colors."

"Thanks, yeah, well we, Brad and I, were taught a lot of things. It's been a long time since I had the chance to put any of it into practice. In the last few months, I've been trying to help my mom, by myself." She placed her own napkin beside her plate and Terri waited for her to finish. "You can't imagine, how lousy it made me feel, when I would set her a nice tray because *she just could not get out of bed* and she would, *literally* throw it right back at me." Brianna laughed a little but then sounded bitter, again. "She scared Louise away, you know. Annette is just barely hanging in there. I think she was waiting for me to turn 18, so she knew I could get away if I wanted to. Now, I can. Where I go from here, is anyone's guess. I definitely have some thinking to do." Brianna took another sip of her coffee and sighed.

Terri picked up her mug then, pushed back from the table and filled it, adding cream and sugar. She offered the pot to Brianna, who accepted the refill.

"Let's go sit in the living room," Terri said. "I have an idea, that I want to talk to you about." Brianna looked intrigued, as they moved to the sofa.

Louie and Maria, who had been dozing as the girls ate, woke-up and started playing, as the two girls sat down with their coffee. Brianna put down her cup and buried her face in Maria's luxuriant fur, while Terri grabbed Louie, so he wouldn't feel neglected. Terri hadn't realized how much attention these two had needed. It definitely made a difference in their behavior. They hadn't gotten into any trouble for the last couple of days, with all the pampering they were getting. Now, Terri looked at Brianna and tried to explain what she had in mind.

"Brianna," she put down her mug and asked her, "do you know what I do, as a chef, I mean?"

"Well, my grandpa told me you work at a Supper Club, *Twin Pines*, right? That's how he first got to know you and Angie. You work there and Angie is your best friend, the cop. I guess I figured, you were a chef there. Aren't you?" Brianna looked confused, now.

"I help out in the kitchen, at *Twin Pines* but no, I am not one of the chefs, on the staff at the restaurant. I have already taken some courses in food service and I am taking a couple of marketing classes, here in Boston. The way I make most of my living now, is by being a personal chef." Brianna waited for an explanation of what was involved. "I have, at the moment, six families for which I prepare four dinners a week. It's a lot of work and I have been thinking about taking on an assistant for some time. Captain Mathews, told me yesterday, that he thinks I have good instincts. My instincts are telling me now, that *you* would make a great assistant. Do you think you might be interested? If you would like to consider it, think about it, or whatever, not only could we have a great time but I could take on more clients, if I had your help." She looked at Brianna and saw surprise, along with interest.

"Wow," Brianna said, as she took another sip of her coffee. Terri waited for her young friend, to absorb what she had proposed. "I would have to talk to my dad about it. I know what my mom would say, so I don't think I'll worry about her, for now. She seems to be getting taken care of anyway, finally by someone besides me."

Brianna thought for another minute and then asked Terri to explain, exactly what she did. Terri went into great detail, telling Brianna, about her families and described some of the food she made. She also explained, that she used the kitchen of the *Twin Pines* and how this arrangement, had come about. They were still discussing it, when they heard a tap on the door and Angie's usual greeting.

"Hey, hey, is everybody up?" Angie came in, with her key, like always and the cats jumped off the sofa, to run up and greet her. "What's going on, here, some kind of a pow-wow?" She went into the kitchen, grabbed a mug and filled it, with the still hot coffee. Terri and Brianna waited now, until Angie had settled onto the other end of the sofa and then explained what they had been discussing. Angie thought that it was a fantastic idea and was as impressed as Terri, when she heard about the breakfast Brianna had prepared.

"Well, Brianna," Angie said and looked wickedly at Terri, "I hope she doesn't barf it up, like she did when I made omelets, yesterday."

"Angie!" Terri started scolding her pal and then, only because she finally felt better, she played along. "Well, that would *only* be if Captain Mathews shows up, like he did yesterday morning."

"Oh, and he *has* to be wearing the uniform," Angie interjected into the horse play, "don't forget the uniform. How come I never get that kind of a reaction, when I wear mine? What's up with that, anyway?"

"Oh, I don't know," Terri thought about this question. "You might be surprised at the reaction you get, Angie. It's just that, when you *are* wearing your uniform, there's always too much going on around you, for you to notice."

"Oh, really?" Angie was interested now. "Would you like to give me *a for instance?*"

Brianna watched them and finally surmised the situation. "You guys are nuts, do you know that?" She was amazed at how much she was enjoying their company.

"Oh, we've never denied that charge," agreed Angie and Terri laughing, said, "Stop, my head hurts, again."

"You know, you guys," Brianna sobered then and looked kind of ashamed, "I have never had a real job. Can you imagine? Most of the kids in school did something. They babysat, or the guys mowed lawns or did yard work. Even some of the so-called *rich kids*, had parents that had enough common sense, to make their kids start to work, *somewhere*. I never could because of my mother." Then she brightened and made up her mind. "That's it," Brianna said, firmly, "I am 18 years old and can make my own decisions. Terri I would love to work for you and with you. Let's shake on it!" She put out her hand and they shook vigorously.

"Congratulations!" Angie said, whole heartedly. "I'll drink to that!" She said taking a sip of the strong coffee. "Ah, just the way I like it."

"Brianna made it," Terri said, " and here's to many cups of coffee to come." She held up her coffee and they all clanked their mugs together. "All for one, and one for all!" Terri, who of course was thrilled with Brianna's decision, made an enthusiastic toast. Brianna started laughing again.

"Did you make that up?" Angie asked, with a straight face.

"Oh, yeah, of course, just now," Terri said and Brianna almost spit out her coffee.

"The Three Musketeers, we ain't !" Angie said, thinking about the movie, "but can I be the Kiefer Sutherland, guy? Man, he is so hot! I can't wait for 24 to start, again."

"Ah, yes, another terrible day in the life of *Jack Bauer*. How can we resist?" Terri sighed. "I could just sit and listen to *his voice*, all day! Previously, on 24......" she started, with a *not very* convincing imitation of the voice.

"What are you guys talking about, anyway?" Brianna asked, totally confused, again.

"O.K.," said Terri, looking at her sympathetically, "I was wrong. Your education, in this case, has been *truly neglected*, if you have not gone through a season of *24*. It gets a little intense but....." Before Terri could finish, Brianna's cell phone chirped.

"Oh, it's my dad! Daddy," she said into her phone, "so how's Mom?"

Brianna went into the bedroom to talk privately with her father, giving Terri and Angie a few minutes alone.

"So, aside from the fact that, suddenly you have a brand new, obviously talented, young assistant, how are feeling? I promise, after this week-end, I will not ask you that question, *ever again*. We have the game tonight, so you need to be in tip-top shape!" Angie said, trying to be encouraging.

"It's O.K., Ang.," Terri said, "I *am* feeling, like a hundred times better. You have no idea how relieved I am, knowing I have an assistant, *finally*. It's been bugging me for ages. I have at least, a half dozen more families on a waiting list and I've been holding them off, trying to figure out, how or if, I was going to find someone to help me or just tell them to forget it. It is a huge relief and as weird as the last couple of days have been, all that has happened, has worked out for the best."

"O.K., so how did you make this decision so fast?" Angie asked, sipping her coffee and heading back to the kitchen for a warm-up. Then, seeing the coffee pot was nearly empty, she proceeded to make a fresh one.

Terri told Angie about how Brianna had fixed breakfast, set the table and the way she had obviously been taught, to have wonderful table manners. Terri knew good training when she saw it and Brianna had been trained, very well. Angie was also impressed and agreed that Terri had made a good choice.

Brianna came out of the bedroom, finally to tell the girls what was happening. "My dad will be here, in about an hour or so. I gave him your address, Terri. He is going to leave the loaner car here and then it'll get picked up by the car rental company. Will that be O.K?"

Terri assured Brianna that would be fine. There was a parking lot, behind Terri's building. She was able to park her truck, in the alley, by her outside stairs.

"Oh, and by the way you guys," Brianna looked at them pointedly, "I know that my mother *attempted suicide*." She put exaggerated finger quotes around the words 'attempted suicide' and Terri and Angie were surprised, to say the least. "This is not the first time." Brianna went on to explain. "If she really wanted to take her own life, she would have done it by now. It's an attention getter, according to the doctors. She has made a couple of attempts but only when she knows someone will find her. She took a bunch of pills one time and called my dad, just to get him to come home and feel sorry for her." She plopped on the couch, grabbed a comfy pillow and held it tightly to her tummy. Maria, of course, hopped on the pillow and looked at Brianna mournfully. "Look at her face," said Brianna, as she caressed the sympathetic animal, "what is it about cats and dogs, anyway? They actually know when you're down. Ever notice that, Terri?"

"Oh, absolutely!" Terri agreed. "The first day I was home, after getting this," she pointed at the bump, "they knew right away something weird was up. Of course, they got over it pretty fast, 'cause when I got up the next morning, they were hanging out with Angie. They're so resilient, just like little kids. They can adapt to almost any situation and go on their instincts. We grown-up humans, on the other hand, are supposed to use our brains, *hopefully*, along *with* our instincts."

"Mmmm," Angie now said, pretending to ponder, "ever since Rico told Terri, she has good instincts, that's all she can talk about." She rolled her eyes and sighed, with her hand on her heart.

"Angie, shut-up!" Terri kicked at her. "Why is it, once again, I feel like we are warping back to Jr. High? Can we concentrate on what's going on, here? Stop talking about Rico for awhile, Angie. There isn't a damn thing going on between him and me, at this point. Man, *I wish there was!* Until this ridiculous murder has been solved, we can not go anywhere with anything else."

"O.K., fine, you're right. I will not tease you anymore, at least until this murder is solved." Angie reluctantly, agreed to that much but went off on another subject. "Oh, and isn't it, him and I or is it, he and I? Who was your English teacher, anyway? I thought that was your subject. Sure as hell wasn't mine," she wrinkled her nose, just thinking about it.

"Whatever!" Terri said, "We both had the same English teacher as everyone else and everyone else, since. I loved him, by the way and he's still there, good old J.C. *My Mom*, actually had him for a teacher, when she started High School in 1968. She always tells the story about, how she made this really cool term paper on the Beatles and how much she loved it. Well, one day, she walked into class and he had taken it apart and made a bulletin board out of it! She still talks about it because she was so traumatized. Can you imagine, if she still had that term paper? At least someone could have recycled that baby!"

"Well, at least anyone, who doesn't go to the same high school we did," Angie added.

By now, Brianna was looking at both of them, like they had completely lost their minds. "What?" both Terri and Angie asked at the same time.

"What in the hell are you guys talking about?" Brianna started to get excited now. "Terri, how old is your mother, anyway? I mean, 1968? For crying out loud, that's like the Vietnam War and stuff! Did she ever *meet* the Beatles, or anything? That's pretty cool, when you think about it. Did she go to Woodstock? I heard that was pretty cool, too."

"As a matter of fact," Terri informed her, "she did *not* meet the Beatles. I really don't think many of the fans did. She was only in 4th grade, when they hit the shores of this country. Also, she *did not* go to Woodstock, she was only 14, at the time. She's just going to be 51, this fall. She never did any of the heavy drugs, they did back then, fortunately. Drank a lot though, I guess, when she was going with my dad. That's what they did back then, *hell*, it was the 70's! She always says, she's amazed, they made it out of that weird decade, alive. O.K., now we just crossed back over to the original problem, sorry Bri. Hey, is it alright if I call you that? I like it, suits you, if it's O.K." Terri said, finishing her history lesson and trying to get away from any discussion of drugs and alcohol.

"Of course, it's O.K., if you call me Bri. That's what people call me, pretty much." Brianna started wrestling with Maria, who had a pretty strong grip on her arm and was starting to nibble. "*Oww!*, O.K., little girl, enough of that! You're getting way too rough," she scolded and bumped the cat onto the floor. Then she thought for a second. "You know Terri, you are so lucky that your mom stopped drinking and never got into drugs. It must be great to have a mom like that."

"Yeah, *it is* great to have a mom like mine," Terri said, trying hard to concentrate on how fortunate she was, "but your mom is working on getting better, so keep positive thoughts. Don't give up." She tried to sound encouraging. Angie, thinking about her own mom, had nothing to add, as she sipped her coffee.

"I won't give up," Brianna agreed to that much, "at least not yet." Then she looked at her watch. "Man, we've been talking and my Dad will be here in a few minutes. She got up to get her stuff together. "Oh Terri," Brianna stopped then and asked, "when do you want me to start working with you? I told my Dad about our plans and he thinks it is a great idea. He does want me to take some college courses though, just in case I want to do something else but he knows how much I love to cook, so who knows? Oh, and I have some great ideas for recipes, chicken Cordon Bleu, beef stroganoff, beef Wellington. Oh, Louise showed me how to make all kinds of really wonderful things and I always paid close attention. I....." Terri finally stopped her.

"O.K., Brianna, you've got me convinced. Can you come back here, to Boston tomorrow, so you can start fixing meals with me, on Monday morning?" Terri asked, hopefully, knowing how great it would be to finally have the help she had been needing.

"Absolutely, I can't wait!" Brianna agreed happily and they toasted, once again with their coffee cups. "All for one...." she started...

"....and one for all!," the three friends said together. "Alexander Dumas would be proud!" Angie said, adding her approval.

Chapter 14

Brianna's father picked her up at around 12:00 noon. Hurrying to get on with the rest of her life, Brianna saw him drive up, grabbed her bag and ran out the door, promising Terri she would be back tomorrow afternoon.

Terri saw her off with relief, but *what a find this girl was!* She couldn't wait to get her started, on Monday morning. She also felt more than a little relieved, not to meet David Severson, quite yet. She felt disturbed and opinionated about how he had thus far ignored his family. Terri hated being judgmental and she rarely was but seeing how it affected young Brianna, was just really hard to take. Well, hopefully this would be the start of some big changes for all of them. Brianna was Terri's main focus, for now. David Severson had his wife to deal with and Terri was more than happy, to be able to look after Brianna.

Terri, finally alone for a few hours, spent the rest of the day, catching up with everything she hadn't done all week. First, the murder had hit everyone like a ton of bricks. Terri had gone to her classes anyway, despite everything. Even though it was difficult to concentrate, she couldn't afford to miss any of them. Then there was the funeral, followed by the disastrous visit to Ed's house.

Terri, on the other hand, continued to think, with everything that had happened, she could handle the concussion. She had met Rico and even though they where *just friends* she would settle for that, *for now*. Some of the best, long lasting relationships, were based on being friends first. Also, even though Brianna turned out to be the one in Ed's house, she not only had another good friend, she had a great, new assistant.

Terri proceeded to do four loads of laundry and call her order to Jack. She needed some special cheeses, for next week, to go with the meats she still had at *Twin Pines*. Even though she had left sample menus as usual, with her clients, she always reserved the right to make changes. Now that she had Brianna helping her, they could try some different recipies, starting with the beef stroganoff or maybe the chicken Cordon Bleu. She certainly had the meats for both. They also would need to shop for stuff on the side, such as, sour cream, noodles and of course, fresh produce, first thing on Monday morning. When Brianna got back to Terri's apartment tomorrow afternoon, they would settle her, and whatever she brought with her, into Terri's spare room. She would stay with Terri, until they could find her an apartment of her own.

In the meantime, Terri had the game to get ready for. The four women were set to take a taxi to the restaurant and then, take another after dinner, to Fenway Park. It was 4:00 and Terri needed to take her shower and figure out which one of her dozens of Red Sox t-shirts, with a pair of red shorts, that she would wear to the game, along with a pair of comfortable low-cut tennis shoes.

At exactly 4:45, Terri was out of her apartment door and down the stairs. A block down the street, Amber and Kellie were locking the store. They put up the, **'Sorry, Gone to the Game'**, sign and looking up, Terri saw Angie coming down the sidewalk. Terri had already called the taxi and it was waiting, so they all piled in, laughing and getting into the mood.

At *Al Dente Ristorante*, where they arrived, exactly on time, 5:00, straight up, they were seated almost immediately. First order of business, was a round of drinks. After the wine Terri had drank on Thursday night, the day she had been at Ed's house, she decided to stick with club soda. The last thing she wanted, was to ruin, what would be a wonderful meal, by getting an upset stomach. Angie had her favorite of course, a martini, with three huge olives. Kellie went for a strawberry Tom Collins and Amber chose a wonderful White Zinfandel. Very little was said, as they perused the vast assortment of wonderful choices and slowly savored their drinks.

Suddenly, out of the blue, Angie spoke solemnly. "You know, I worked with this chick at the police station a few years ago. She was pretty cool and really fun to work with. Anyway, she finally retired when she started having grandchildren to hang out with but she was pretty smart about life and used to give me all kinds of good advice." Angie paused for effect and all looked at her, waiting for the magic words of wisdom to come. She finally continued.

"Anyway, *she said,* that with every situation, if possible, you should always keep your sense of humor." All nodded in agreement, that being good advice. Angie went on. *"She said,* this was important and this is how she said it, *'unless-in someone dies'."*

Or, in the case of Ed, someone is murdered, Terri was thinking and waiting to see if there was a punch line or what. She knew Angie pretty well and she was being way too straight, as she was telling this tale. They all sipped their drinks, as they listened, not suspecting what was to come. Angie finally went on.

" Then she said, she went to this funeral for this really old guy, he was like 102, or something and his name was Mr. Stiff and...." but Angie didn't need to finish. Terri choked on her club soda, Kellie splashed pink liquid out of her Tom Collins and Amber almost shot wine out of her nose. They all started laughing so hard, that everyone in the whole restaurant was looking over at them.

"What?" Angie asked, trying to look innocent and failing badly. Their waiter came over to see if there was a problem. He was also wondering, *if maybe, they had made several stops before they came to this establishment. They hadn't seemed under the weather to him, when they were first seated.* "It's O.K., it's O.K.,"

Terri assured the confused young man and why wouldn't he be? It was pretty early in the evening to be this goofy. "My friend, here," she gestured to Angie, " just told us a funny story and it was a little on the unexpected side....," she was still laughing and wiping away the tears. Angie tried to pretend innocence but finally gave up. Their waiter was no snob and said he would give them a little more time.

"Maybe you should tell me the story," he said, gamely, "I sure could use a good laugh, today. But don't wait too long, you don't want to miss the first pitch." He smiled and scurried away, after they assured him, they would make up their minds presently and thanked him for his patience.

"O.K., c'mon you guys," said Terri, trying to sound stern, "Angie, for God's sake, where did you get that silly story? There is no way some guy had the last name of Stiff! Geez!"

"No, honest, that is a true story, at least Ruth told me it was. That was her name, Ruth Schmitz. She said the guys' name was Roy Stiff and she was dead serious. Whoops, sorry!" They all started to laugh, again.

"Enough!" Terri hissed. "Let's order. Man, I'm ravenous! Get a hold of yourselves! Appetizers, yes?" They all agreed and Terri signaled to their anxious but amused waiter.

"Everybody O.K., now?" he asked with a friendly smile.

"Everything is great," Terri assured him, "and we would like a couple of appetizers, to share. Alright if I order, ladies?" She gave her dining companions a warning look, as if to say, *"Behave, before they bounce us out of here!"*

Angie gave her a strained, somber glance. "Please do," she answered, very properly, as Kellie and Amber nodded, somberly.

They started with Bruschetta and the Mussels Marinara. Their waiter hurried away with their order for 'starters' and another round of drinks.

Terri was more glad than ever, that she was sticking with club soda and probably a coke, at Fenway. She was already starting to get a little whoosy, still from the clunk on the head and probably because she needed to eat.

Presently, the appetizers were on the table and they dug in, enjoying them immensely. Sounds of, *mmmmm...and yummy,* all around, pleased their waiter to no end, as he had now taken a personal interest in them.

By the time they finally ordered the main course, shrimp scampi for Terri and Kellie, linguine with clam sauce for Angie and chicken marsala for Amber, they had pretty much settled down. They had also enjoyed a wonderful minestrone, along with buttery garlic bread. Their waiter, who had introduced himself as Joseph when they sat, was professional but friendly, thus making the service perfect, as well as enjoyable. They left him a very generous tip, split the bill and bugged out, for the game.

Checking the time on her cell phone, Terri saw that it was 6:30. After all that goofing off, they still had plenty of time to get to Fenway Park. The hostess at Al Dente, had called them a taxi and it was waiting when they went outside. It was a gorgeous night. Angie looked up at the sky, though.

"I think it's going to rain tomorrow," she said, "I'm glad we're catching a game tonight."

They all piled into the taxi and scrunched in, Angie in the front with the startled cabbie.

"Hey, don't worry," she assured him, with a stifled belch, after the wonderful meal, "I'm a cop, so you're safe with us! To the ballpark, James," she said pointing in the general direction of Fenway, *"and step on it!* Uh, I mean, get us there in one piece."

They all started giggling again, with only a little less control than at dinner and the cab driver shook his head. *It takes all kinds,* he thought and away they went.

They saw a wonderful game. The Chicago White Sox were in town and the Red Sox won, 7 to 4. At one point, a foul ball, off the bat of Johnny Damon whizzed over the top of Terri's head. It ended up in the hands of a very happy, twelve year old boy however, so she wasn't too upset about it. She just had to remember to always **DUCK!!!**

They had so much fun, that all the weird stuff that had happened within the last few days, was temporarily off their minds. Everybody, except Terri, of course, had a couple of beers. So, by the time they piled back into another taxi and headed for home, they were all exhausted.

They talked about the Sox' chances of going back to the Series again, since they were looking pretty good.

"I could handle it," exclaimed Angie, "look how many times *them Damn Yankees* have taken it. Two years in a row would be awesome."

"Well, I don't know," put in Kellie, "the White Sox are actually looking pretty good. Wouldn't it be nice, if they could go ahead and *reverse their curse* too, ya' know? Just get it out of the way, like our guys did? I think they have a real chance."

"You traitor!" Angie, who had imbibed in probably one too many beers during the game, was totally freaked. "How can you say that?"

"I can say that," explained Kellie patiently, "because I love the game. If you love the game, you can be loyal to your own team but also appreciate, if someone else gets a chance and I think the White Sox deserve a chance."

"Yeah, and my favorite Uncle, your Dad, resides in Chicago and lives and breathes the White Sox!" Amber revealed, getting a punch from her cousin. "Ah, hah!" Angie jumped on this, "the truth comes out!"

"*You can't handle the truth!*" Kellie shot back, laughing and at that Terri jumped in.

"O.K., that's it, discussion over. If I hear one more bad movie line, today, I will certainly barf, again," she threatened.

"What?" Their cabbie shrieked, "don't you be hurling in my cab, lady!"

"It's O.K., " said Terri, "just kidding, just kidding. Just get us to our block and if I have to hurl, I'll hurl outside."

With that, the cabbie stepped on the gas and they all flew back in their seats. They were back home in no time flat!

Terri felt like she had lead in her feet, as she climbed the stairs to her door and waved to her friends, who were laughing and walking down the street to their respective apartments. It was nice to all live so close together and enjoy each others company, the way they did. Terri lived alone but she never felt alone. Also, when she unlocked her door and went in, Louie and Maria met her with enthusiastic greetings. Terri was so tired however, she barely managed to brush her teeth, change into her P.J.s and fall into bed, before she was sound asleep, with the cats at her feet.

Sunday morning, at 8:30, her cell phone rang in an incredibly annoying fashion and Terri groaned as she rolled over, on to Louie no less, to grab it and stop the noise. It turned out to be an overly excited Brianna, calling to let Terri know, she had packed up a bunch of her stuff and would be at her apartment by 1:00 or so. David Severson, had actually given Brianna full ownership of the Lincoln, much to Brianna and Terri's delight. Having the truck for the business, was one thing but actually having a car, would be wonderful. So far, young Brianna had proved to be a very responsible and reliable asset, to Terri's life. Elizabeth was doing better but she would be hospitalized for some time. Brianna truly cared for her mother but she was so happy at the prospect of not having to worry about and be responsible for her anymore, that she couldn't wait to get back to Boston and her new life. Terri heartily agreed with her, hung up and set her alarm for 10:30. If she didn't get a couple more hours of sleep, she'd never get anything done. After a quick trip to the bathroom, she burrowed back under the covers for awhile, so Louie and Maria, left her to it.

Chapter 15

Terri hadn't been up five minutes, when her phone rang, the land-line again. Her mother no doubt, she thought and walked over to the cordless, first taking a look at the caller I.D. Oh great, a *blocked number* but on a Sunday morning? Instincts kicking in once more, she picked up the phone, instead of ignoring it, and answered with a polite, hello?

"Terri." There was that voice again and as she felt a painful but excited lurch in her stomach, Terri let Rico Mathews' face come to her mind. The brown eyes, the dark wavey hair and he smelled so good, he….."Terri!" Rico sounded alarmed, "Are you there, or not?" *Well, now that was a silly question, if there ever was one. Who would have answered the phone?*

"Yes, I'm here, sorry Rico," she warmed to using his name. *They weren't at the police station at the moment, so she could do that. Yeah!* "There's been a lot going on, since we last spoke. So, how are you?" *Oh, brilliant conversation style there Terri, real original.* She was relieved once again, that he couldn't see her screwing up her face, through the telephone line. *Would she ever be comfortable with this person?*

"Me?, Hey, no complaints. I wanted to apologize for running off so fast the other day. It was a family emergency, that I couldn't avoid." *Oh well, good thing that's cleared up,* Terri thought. *Well, it really was none of her damn business anyway!* Still, she couldn't help feeling a little bit at a loss.

"Anyway, we need to get back to this investigation. I really want to clear this up. Do you, by any chance, know how I can get in touch with Brianna? She really needs to get back down here, so I can ask her some questions." Rico finished the explanation for his call and Terri's disappointment, felt worse than the bump on her head. As a matter of fact, *she would have rather had another concussion, than this let down. Then again, maybe not, she thought, always practical.*

"Oh well, yes," Terri recovered the best she could, "she was here with me Friday night. Her father picked her up yesterday and she's coming back here this afternoon." Terri had intended to launch into what was happening, with her and Brianna but Rico seemed distracted and jumped in before she could go any further.

"That's great! Would it be possible to have her down here at the station, tomorrow afternoon, say around 1:30?" Terri said that would be fine, trying not to sound like she had just been punched in the gut. "Being away, the last couple of days, my morning is full, paper work and stuff," Rico said quickly. "See you ladies tomorrow afternoon then."

"Rico, I....." Terri helplessly tried to keep things moving but she was holding a dead phone and a dead end. "Oh, for crying out loud!" Terri said, looking at the two, as usual, clueless cats. "What is up with this guy, anyway?" Louie and Maria had no answers for her and she placed the phone back on the charger. She sighed and headed for the bathroom.

Terri had paper work of her own to do, so after coffee, toast and tomato juice, she spent a couple of hours, making lists, paying bills and filing invoices. She always fished through the Sunday paper, checking grocery store prices and looking at adds for yard sales. She had no clue what Brianna would be bringing with her and since the extra bedroom was not that big, hopefully they would find her an apartment, in the next couple of weeks. That being the case, she also checked the classifieds, for *flats to rent.* It would be good if they could keep her close. Terri would have to spread the word around, that they were looking. That usually seemed to be the best way to get things done.

Angie called at about 1:00 and Terri told her about the conversation with Rico. "I gotta tell you, Ang," Terri said, exasperated, "this guy is starting to get under my skin. Does he ever do anything but work? It's Sunday, for Pete's sake and he called me *from the station!* I guess you're right," she said, close to tears, "maybe he just won't ever do anything, anymore but his job. *This sucks!*"

"I'm sorry, Terri," Angie really did feel bad for her friend, "but this is what I was telling you about, from the beginning. He called me, too. Woke me up, *the shit!* At least you didn't have one too many beers at Fenway last night. You were the smart one. I feel like crap!" Angie whined.

Of course, she got no sympathy from Terri. "Serves you right," she said, in her best scolding voice, "you know you can't drink, anymore. Sheez, I never could. I feel hung over, if I don't get enough sleep. I'm totally bummed, right now. O.K., so *why did you call me, or did I call you?* Right now, I can't remember." Terri put her hand on her head and leaned on her desk.

"Geez, I thought I was in bad shape!" Angie laughed now. "Allow me to enlighten you. I called you to find out if Brianna was there, yet. What's going on, anyway? Also, Judith wants us to come over for dinner tonight and you know what that means!"

Terri groaned. "Oh, Angie, I don't know if I can. Besides, what about Brianna? I can't just leave her here, by herself, on her first night in Boston."

"Got that covered. She's invited, too. Oh, and here is the best part. The whole meal, from appetizer to main course and dessert, of course, is all designed around using *chocolate!* What do you make of that?" Angie was enjoying herself, immensely. She knew Terri could not resist such an offer.

"Oh, my God, Angie!" Terri shrieked. "You have got to be kidding!"

"Somehow, I knew what your reaction would be. So, where is Brianna, anyway?" Angie went back to the original question. A knock on her door gave them the answer before Terri could. "She's here!" Terri said, excitedly and Angie hung up, with the promise that she would be over as soon as she showered and dressed. *Showered and dressed, at 1:30, in the afternoon?* Terri shook her head and ran for the door. There was Brianna, with her father behind her looking embarrassed. Terri started laughing, as they were both so loaded down with suitcases and bags, it couldn't help but be comical.

"Well," Terri said, with a grin, as she opened the door. "I see you've come prepared for anything!" She swung the door wide, with a sweeping gesture of welcome.

"I wasn't sure what to bring," Brianna said, dropping a load of bags, right at her feet and moving so David Severson, could come through the door with his arms full. David put down the parcels and bags, he had hauled up the stairs, to the door and put his hand out, to shake Terri's warmly.

"I want to thank-you, so much," he said sincerely, "for all your help. This is amazing, I mean, what you are doing for Brianna. I didn't realize what she was dealing with and I am sorry for that."

Terri didn't know what to say. She didn't want Brianna's father, to think he owed her any kind of an apology but David felt differently. "What you had to put up with from my wife, was inexcusable. She is extremely ill and I must tell you, her problems have been building for a long time, *too long.* Sometimes people have to get to the very bottom, before they get help. Elizabeth reached that point and she is fortunate to be alive and get another chance. Well, we have talked about my wife enough. The important thing now, is my daughter." He hugged her close and Brianna sighed with happiness.

"Thanks, Daddy," she said, "I know I will be fine here, with Terri and Angie. Oh, and look at these two," she dropped down to play with the fluffy kitties, who had run to the door, when the company came in. "Aren't they adorable, Daddy?"

Brianna buried her face in their fur and they basked in the attention.

David Severson cleared his throat and Terri looked at him, trying to suppress another laugh. Either you liked cats or you didn't and Terri suspected that he didn't. "Uh, actually, I'm more of a dog person, myself but yes, they are beautiful, Honey. They certainly seem to like you already, Bri," he observed, dryly.

"Oh, they pretty much like anyone who wants to spoil them with attention and that would be Brianna," Terri agreed.

"O.K., well this looks very nice," David observed, scanning the apartment quickly. "This is certainly a very good location. I also understand Terri, your best friend is a police officer. Is that right?" Obviously, he asked the question, still concerned for his daughter's welfare and Terri took that concern, seriously.

"That is correct, sir," Terri said firmly, "my friend Angie, who is indeed, a police officer, lives just a couple of blocks down from here. Also, our good friends, Amber and Kelli, own and run the health food store, just down the block. I have lots of great connections, especially in business and in food service. You can feel comfortable, leaving Brianna here. Angie and I will take excellent care of her."

"You don't have to worry, Daddy!" Brianna said. "I'll be safe here with Terri. Then eventually, Angie and Terri, will help me find my own place. I don't mind staying with Terri and the kitties, for awhile though. We better get the rest of my stuff out of the car, so you can get going."

Terri could see Brianna was anxious to reasure her father but she wanted to get him quickly on his way.

"I'll help you!" Terri said, wondering how much more stuff Brianna had brought. They all started back down the stairs.

David Severson took out his cell phone. "I need to call the rental company and make sure my car is on the way, as I will be leaving the Lincoln with you girls. Do you have a driver's license, Terri?"

"Yes, this is my truck I use for my business," Terri said, gesturing to the vehicle next to her staircase. David nodded, and started talking into his cell phone.

Terri looked at Brianna like, *what the...?* Brianna gave her a buggy-eyed stare that said, *let's just get him out of here!* They both started grabbing more bags out of the car.

By the time they got all of Brianna's belongings, or at least what she had brought with her, up into the apartment, David's rental car had arrived. Brianna gave her father a quick hug good-bye. Terri and Brianna flopped down onto the sofa and looked at the mess. Louie and Maria circled around the pile of bags and stuffed animals, sniffing and investigating. Finding nothing of interest to them, the curious cats, joined the girls on the sofa and waited to see what they would do.

"You guys are really lazy, you know that?" Terri observed, as Louie and Maria, flopped down for another one of their twenty or so naps, that day. "Oh man, I have had next to nothing to eat today. No wonder I feel so horrible!" Terri looked at Brianna and said one more word. "Hungry?"

"Oh yeah!" Brianna was right behind Terri as they headed for the kitchen to investigate the fridge, for something quick. They came up with sliced honey-smoked turkey, romaine lettuce and Swiss cheese slices, and a wonderful brown, German mustard. Terri had Kaiser rolls and baked potato chips. Along with fresh lemonade, they were set.

"Oh Terri, this is wonderful," said Brianna, after a couple bites of the delicious sandwich. "You just have the best food to make anything. Where did you get this turkey? It is fabulous!"

"Wait until you meet Jack, my butcher. I get the best of everything from him because *he has the best of everything.* Also, um.....Brianna, what do you have for money? You may be here for awhile and there's rent, food, utilities, you know." Terri felt uncomfortable bringing up the subject.

"Oh yeah, I know," Brianna came back quickly, surprising Terri, yet again, as she went on. "No problem. You want to hear the really sad part? I have money. I have more money than you can *ever* imagine. When I turned 18, I got a huge pay-off from my trust fund. When I turn 21, I'll get an even bigger one. I can buy anything I want and anything *you* need. Daddy will deny me nothing. Especially, since I have never given him any reason, to think I was spending money recklessly. I don't drink, of course, or do drugs, or buy tons of clothes and jewelry. I watched my mother do all that." The bitterness in her voice helped Terri to understand, what Brianna had been through, as she continued.

"My mother shopped, did so-called, *party drugs*, with her stupid friends. She redecorated the house, like a million times. I told you already, how she wrecked at least a half dozen vehicles. She actually rolled a Beamer and walked away from it! I was so disgusted. I mean, I didn't want her to die but she just never learned her lesson because it never hit her hard enough." Brianna stopped talking, looked at Terri's shocked face and took another bite of her sandwich. "Mmmm, yummy," she said and wiped mustard from the corner of her mouth. "Aren't you going to say anything?"

"Um, well, Brianna, I don't know what to say. You seem so grounded, so down to earth. I guess there I go, stereo-typing again. I'm sorry." Terri wasn't sure what to think, now. She took another bite of sandwich and munched on a chip.

"Yeah, well there's a lot of spoiled rich kids out there and I ain't one of 'em. So, O.K. Terri, here is what I propose. I have to say it, no matter how it sounds. I don't need money. I don't *have* to work, *ever* but I *want* to work. I need the experience. I need your friendship, yours and Angie's. I would like to get to a couple of Red Sox games with you guys. I want to take some classes. Do you know if I can still sign up for the Fall semester? I want to....", Brianna was cut off, however, by Angie's usual greeting as she came through the door.

"Hey, what's up?" Angie came into the kitchen, grabbed a Kaiser roll and started putting together her own sandwich.

"What's up?" Terri asked, with her arms folded over her chest. She was stunned by Brianna's words and couldn't imagine Angie's reaction. "Well, *besides you, finally*, as you may have noticed when you walked in, we have some work to do. Also, Brianna was just telling me what kind of arrangements, she would like to make for our living situation *and for our* business relationship. Brianna, pray continue." Terri gave the floor back to Brianna and Angie looked at her and Terri, expectantly.

"Well, anyway, as I was telling Terri, I don't want to work for money. I have money. I want to learn and hang out with you guys. I guess I should be with kids my own age, I mean I am still a teenager but it just seems like they are still so immature. I want to start to live and *not* have to put up with anymore of the crap, I've had to deal with for the last 10 years. *Can you believe that?* I have been taking all this bullshit, from my mother, *for 10 years!* What a waste!" Brianna, suddenly looked stricken. Terri and Angie looked at each other. *Was Brianna going to be alright?*

Brianna saw the look between the two women. "Hey, you guys, I'll be fine. I'm better than ever. I had almost given up before this all happened. Anyway, what I was proposing Terri, is this. You do not have to pay me. I'll live here, help you pay for food and take care of the apartment. I also know how to clean and I can help you take care of the kitties. I want you guys to teach me everything, how to cook, how to live. We will have a blast, anything you want, anything you need, *you've got it,* courtesy of Daddy."

Terri and Angie looked at each other, with a *can you believe this?* look.

"Uh, Brianna, you don't have to buy us stuff," said Terri. "You stay here with me and I can keep you plenty busy enough, to make up for rent and we can shop for food, together. How does that sound?"

"That sounds like a plan," Brianna said, satisfied with their agreement. This time, they clinked glasses of tangy lemonade and finished lunch, so they could tackle and somehow organize, Brianna's belongings. While they did this, Angie mentioned, that they were invited for dinner, over to her dad's house.

"Your dad cooks?" Brianna asked, amazed once again, about all the new experiences she was having.

"Well, yes but mostly he just barbecues. It's his wife, I guess you could call her my step-mom but I don't really feel like that about her. She's more like a good friend. My mom died about eight years ago, from breast cancer. My dad married Judith, about five years ago and she is a wonderful cook. Except, she likes to serve corresponding wines with each course, so I hope that's not a problem for you, Brianna." Angie looked with concern, at their new friend.

"Not a problem, I can stick with soda or water," said Brianna, as she placed stuffed animals, a teddy here and a lamb there, on to her new bed. She had brought her own pillows and puffy comforter, along with pink sheets and pillow cases. There was of course, an empty bookcase, in the extra room and Brianna filled it, with some of the classics and Terri noticed, several very good cookbooks. She had also brought some photos, in nice frames and a couple of photo albums.

"O.K., if I look at these?" asked Terri, holding the albums.

"Sure," said Brianna, as they plopped on the bed. "It's mostly pictures of me and Brad, with my parents. Wasn't my mother pretty? She still could be, but she's so messed up, she doesn't bother to take care of herself, anymore." They paged through the albums and it was true. Elizabeth Severson, had indeed been very pretty. What had happened to this once, very attractive, woman? When she had confronted Angie and Terri at Cal's house, Elizabeth looked as if she hadn't washed or combed her hair or taken any interest in her personal appearance, for some time. Terri had noticed this, right away. It drove her nuts if someone didn't have clean hair. They had been so shocked, however by her confrontational attitude, the way Elizabeth looked, had been put into the background.

"How old is your mother, Brianna?" Angie asked.

"She is only 42 years old and yes, I know, she looks much older," Brianna said, sadly now. "That is what smoking and drinking will do to a person and by smoking, I don't just mean cigarettes. Hey, did you guys ever try pot? My mom used to keep it in the house, all the time, for her and her yucky friends. *It smelled like crap!* I never could figure out the draw." Brianna sighed and moved on to the next set of photos. Terri and Angie didn't say anything. Both had tried pot, at one time and felt no reason to continue using it. Terri, especially, was a fierce non-smoker and drove Angie crazy, as she wanted to yell at anyone blowing smoke anywhere in her general vicinity. As it turned out, Brianna didn't seem to really want an answer to her question, so neither Angie or Terri volunteered one.

"Geez," Brianna said suddenly, as she put aside a photo album, "what time is it? Angie, when are your dad and step-mom, expecting us?"

"O.K., it's about 4:30, now" said Angie, "and we should be over to Dad and Judith's by 5:30. I'll run back to my place and change. So Brianna, can we take the Lincoln or what?"

"Now, there is a another silly question, if I ever heard one," answered Brianna. "Since you would be the most adept at driving in your wonderful city of Boston traffic Angie, you can pilot!"

"Awesome," said Angie. "I will be the chauffer, to our sumptuous meal. Oh, and did I mention, Brianna, all of the courses are centered around the use of chocolate?"

"What? You have got to be kidding me!" Brianna could not have been more thrilled. "Let me at it! Oh, and do we *dress for dinner?*" she asked, trying to put in a note of high class snobbery.

"We do, indeed," said Angie and she and Terri laughed.

Chapter 16

Dressing for dinner at George and Judith Perry's home meant, Terri borrowed Brianna one of her better Red Sox t-shirts. Both girls wore jean shorts and sandals. Angie, along with her Sox tee, red shorts and comfy scuffs, made up the casual trio, ready to relax and enjoy. Angie piloted the Lincoln safely to Beacon Hill, where George and Judith lived, in one of the smaller but still classic homes. They both greeted Brianna with open arms and a cool soda. Terri and Angie, anticipating several wines, with the elaborate meal, opted for cold glasses of ginger ale. Brianna would stick to soda, of course. Judith and George were also casual and comfortable. George, in a Red Sox button down jersey, with khaki shorts, was not only happy to see his daughter but also Terri, who he considered as close as his own. He greeted Brianna with a friendly pat on the shoulder and asked her what her plans were, now that she was here in Boston. Judith looked cool and comfortable, in light weight, lime green slacks and a sleeve-less, lighter green, silk blouse.

"It is always so nice to have you girls here," Judith said, warmly. "I can't wait to try one of my dinners on your new friend." She gave Brianna a friendly hug and an appraisal. "Good grief, you girls!" Judith said, suddenly. "You did not tell me this girl was so young! You had just better give us the whole story of how you all met. I would assume, it has something to do with the murder of that *awful* Ed Stone," she said with a grimace.

"Now, Judi," said George, "we do not know if that is true. You know how people gossip. What's the story Angie, or can't you tell us?"

"Well, some things I can tell you, Dad and some things I can't," said Angie cautiously. "One thing I can say is, yeah, Judith is right. This guy was into some bad stuff, with some bad people. The investigation seems to be centering around some of his activities, that got him into financial troubles. If he owed people money, they may have whacked him for it!" Angie said, going into cop talk.

"Some of his activities, huh? Oh, you mean like the gambling and boozing? C'mon Angie, you gotta know, I would at least have that much information," George said, looking at his daughter smugly.

"Well, I guess that was kind of common knowledge, anyway," Angie had to admit. "Some people just never grow-up. It's amazing Cal has put up with him all these years."

"Well," Terri, spoke up in Cal's defense, "they have been friends, since they were kids. They went to Korea together. Ed even saved Cal's life, a couple of times. They really cared about one another. Cal tells the stories all the time and he has never said a bad word about Ed. He continues to be as confused about this murder, as the rest of us. Something really wonderful did come out of all this though and that would be finding Brianna, here." Terri put her arm around Brianna's shoulders and the girl smiled with happiness.

"Yes," agreed Judith, "and knowing Terri's excellent judge of character, that is a wonderful thing. We've met your grandfather, Brianna and he is a very nice man." Judith took a sip of her own glass of ginger ale and went on. "Oh well, you girls didn't come over here, to talk about the murder of Ed Stone. Time to try my latest dinner idea, on my favorite guinea pigs. The appetizers are ready. Shall we sit?"

The group moved to the dining area, where they sat at a perfectly set table. Beautiful, gold-rimmed china, crystal glasses and shiny polished real silver, dinner ware, sparkled under soft lighting, on a light gold, table cloth. The silver pieces had been in Judith's family, through at least three generations and she was fiercly proud of and took excellent care of them.

The first course was, cocoa-crusted shrimp with basil, placed before them, by Judith, on delicate hors d'oeuvre plates. This was served with a dry Riesling, poured by George, into gorgeous crystal wine goblets. The girls savored the shrimp and slowly sipped the wine. Brianna opted for cold water and also enjoyed this delicious appetizer.

Next, for the second course, Judith served bright, fresh field greens with slivered almonds, chocolate shavings and a Mango chocolate-infused vinaigrette. Along with red onions and bright, red raspberries, the salad was served with a Pinot Grigio. Pinot, of course, had made a popular comeback, with the movie, *Sideways*, which had been carefully analyzed by all wine lovers. It fit perfectly with the fresh salad course.

For the third and main course, they savored chocolate beef stout stew, along with garlic, mashed potatoes and crisp, green beans. With the delicious beef, they tasted a white Shiraz, which naturally, fit the tender meat, superbly. Terri watched Judith, watching Brianna. It was obvious, both George and Judith, were delightfully impressed with Brianna's impeccable social skills. The way she handled herself and the conversation surrounding the meal, showed Brianna, once again, to be mature beyond her years. Terri still could not get over her good fortune at having found this girl. She and Brianna, would compliment one another perfectly.

All were getting to the point of full and then some, when dessert was served. A gorgeous, raspberry, white chocolate torte, presented on crystal dessert plates, was served with a vintage Port, poured once again by George, into shimmering wine glasses, the fourth in front of their plates.

Dinner finished, they all moved to the living room, to relax. The whole meal had taken exactly two hours, giving them enough time between courses, to feel comfortable for the next. Filling, yet not overly much, it had been a fabulous dinner and

Judith accepted the praise. She also rejected the girls' offer, to help her clean up. She and George would easily put all dishes into their modern, large dish-washer. Judith encouraged all, to relax and let their dinner settle.

"Found it all laid out for me in an old warehouse grocery store catalog, as the perfect Valentine's meal," Judith revealed, "but who needs Valentine's Day to have chocolate? Oh, and I must confess, I did not make the raspberry torte. I had intended to make the chocolate mousse, the menu called for, but when I was shopping for the meal, I saw this torte at my favorite bakery and could not resist. Hope no one minds."

"Not me," said Angie, stifling yet another, huge burp, after the second wonderful meal, in less than 24 hours. "I can't eat another bite, not for the rest of the week. Terri, you and Bri had better pick me up some fresh, veggies, at the market tomorrow. I am on rabbit food, for the next five days."

"Good thing you guys, have me along to drive us back," observed Brianna, as she had watched them all tasting the various wines. "Although, with all the food we just consumed, I would imagine you're fine."

"Not really," said Angie, ever the police officer, "that much alcohol, could put anyone over the legal limit to drive. Why do you think we brought you along? Usually, we stay for the night, as normally we come over on Friday or Saturday. This worked out perfectly!"

"It certainly did," said Terri, patting her tummy. "Oh and I feel wonderful, by the way. No more upset stomachs for me. Judith, as usual, absolutely fabulous! You are a marvelous cook. Even if it *was* laid out in a magazine, you had to put it all together. Oh, and that torte was perfect. You have to tell me which bakery you found it at. Anyway, another success and then some. Thank-you, so much."

Brianna didn't know what to say, she was so amazed with the meal and with George and Judith. She could not have thanked them enough.

By 8:30, Brianna had driven them all safely back home with Angie, side-seat driving of course, in the shot gun position.

Wine or no wine, she could always tell someone where to go and in different ways obviously. Whatever the occasion called for. It was early enough and a nice evening. There had been rain early in the day, actually canceling the baseball game.

"Glad we went to the game last night," commented Angie, "told you it was going to rain."

They had parked the car by Terri's apartment. Now, they were walking with Angie, back to her place, so Brianna could see where she lived. Terri was thinking how, it had been exactly a week, since Ed had been murdered and she suddenly felt a chill. The other two girls noticed Terri shivering, despite the warm summer night and Brianna was startled.

"What's the matter Terri," she asked, with concern for her new boss, "do you have another headache?"

"Terri, what is it?" Angie, grabbed her arm. "Please tell me you are not going to….." but Terri stopped her.

"No, that's not it!" Terri assured her friends. "It's just that, a whole week has gone by and we still do not have a *damn clue*, who murdered Ed." Both of the other girls appeared relieved but Angie agreed.

"Yeah, O.K., I don't blame you. I'm a little freaked out about it, myself. Who ever did this, is still out there, so *that's* never good. I really thought this case would be more simple. You know, as we say, *open and shut?* I can't believe either, that it's still up in the air."

"I wish I could help," put in Brianna. "I can't even imagine what Captain Mathews wants to talk to me about. Do you guys have any idea why I'm being questioned? The whole thing makes me really nervous. I'm not looking forward to going back to that police station tomorrow."

Then before Angie could stop her, Terri spoke up. "All he needs for you to do, Brianna, is account for your mother's whereabouts, on the night of the murder. That would be a week ago, of course. As long as you can do that, it'll be fine." Then she saw Brianna's face, in the street light. All the color had drained from her young friend. Terri grabbed her and suddenly had that sinking feeling again. She knew what was coming before Brianna had a chance to say it.

"I can't!" gasped Brianna.

"You can't, what?" Angie looked stricken.

"I can't account for my Mother's whereabouts, last Sunday night. *We do not know where she was!* She had gotten into the Lincoln, at about 4:00 in the afternoon and taken off. We have no idea where she was, in between then and midnight, when the State Police found her coming back." Brianna had tears running down her cheeks, by this time and buried her face in her hands.

"Damn it!" said Terri.

"Shit!" said Angie.

Chapter 17

A troubled Angie went into her apartment and the last thing she said to the nearly, hysterical Brianna was, "Call your father and have him call your lawyer, *immediately and you did not hear that from me!"*

Brianna hiccupped from crying and looked at Terri. " That sounds like good advice. I have to call my Dad, *now!* Oh, and what did she mean by, *you did not hear that from me?"*

Terri did not feel obliged to answer any questions right then. "C'mon, let's get home!" She grabbed Brianna's hand, they ran back to the apartment and clattered up the stairs. Terri unlocked the door and turned on the lights, as they tripped over the startled Louie and Maria.

"Oh, my God, Terri," Brianna was beside herself, with panic, "my mother could have killed Ed and she may not even remember it. This is nuts, this is totally insane! Should I call my dad, or what? Tell me what to do, please!" Brianna was pleading for help and Terri was stunned. She needed to think for a second and do something normal.

Terri went into the kitchen, got two bottles of cold water out of the fridge and moved Brianna over to the sofa. She picked up the T.V. remote and turned it on. Not much to watch on a Sunday night but somehow, the back round sound just made them both calm down a little. She handed Brianna a bottle of cold *spring water* and tried to sound cool and calm.

"Brianna, first of all," Terri said, as the young girl looked at her, like she was going to fix everything. "Angie gave you some advice and it's sound *but* she really should not be saying anything because of her involvement in this case." Brianna nodded, as that made sense and Terri went on. "I think you should go ahead and call your father, now. I doubt we're breaking any laws, since no one knows where your mother was. We need to see if we can find out, hopefully before tomorrow. She may not have even been anywhere near Boston. So, one thing at a time, O.K.?"

That having been decided, Brianna got on the phone to her father. Terri went to the kitchen once more and put on the teapot. Seemed like as good a time as any, to brew a pot of the Raspberry Midnight Dreams herbal tea, she had purchased at Amber and Kellie's shop. She also had some English biscuits, to go with the tea. After the large meal and the shock of Brianna's revelation about her mother, tea and biscuits would settle their stomachs. Of course, Terri could feel her tummy churning again, so she hoped the tea would help calm her nerves. It would be a crime, to waste Judith's wonderful dinner, if Terri couldn't keep it down.

Terri could hear Brianna talking to David Severson, in hurried, choppy sentences, sometimes raising her voice. Terri could tell, from the little bit of the conversation she could hear, that Brianna was once again, very, very, angry with her mother. The woman seemed to always be getting in the way of Brianna moving on with her life. Finally, Terri heard her say good-bye to her father and the teapot started to whistle.

Brianna came into the kitchen, as Terri got out pretty cups and saucers, along with cream, honey, lemon and biscuits. Terri had poured the boiling water into the pot, that matched the cups and saucers. She had put five of the fragrant tea bags, in the pot, to steep. Terri also placed napkins and spoons on the tray and Brianna carried it out in to the living room. All this was done, without a word having been said between the two girls. They were spent, drained of all energy and spirit. They had been drawn together by tragedy, a brutal murder of a man who, may or may not, have deserved to die. That judgment call could be made by no one, at this point.

A mere week ago, these two young women, separated by more than a decade, hadn't even known one another, yet they felt closer than most life long acquaintances. They both had a vested interest in how this all turned out. It was pretty obvious, that if Elizabeth had murdered Ed, it would have a detrimental effect on Brianna, to say the least.

Terri took the lid off of the pot. They could both smell the raspberry scent wafting out, creating a calming affect, as she stirred the hot liquid with a shiny tea spoon. Brianna put a small amount of cream and lemon into her cup and Terri poured the fragrant tea. Terri put lemon and honey into her cup, poured the hot soothing drink and took a tentative sip. They both picked up and munched on a biscuit. Louie and Maria, had been snoozing on the sofa, of course and roused by the girls, checked the contents of the tray. Once again, finding nothing of interest, they both hopped off the sofa and headed for their bowls.

Terri finally broke the silence. "What did your father say?" she asked, carefully, not laying too much on Brianna, at once.

"He is going to get a hold of our lawyer, tonight. I know the man, of course. He's very good. As I said before, only the best for our family. My mom is not doing well, as expected. She's probably freaking out because she can't have a drink or pills or whatever." Brianna sighed and took another sip of tea, along with a bite of biscuit. "This is so good, Terri," she said, "did you get this at Amber and Kellie's shop?" They needed to talk about something, banal and common place. One way or another, after this was settled, life would go on, more tea would be drank and things would get done.

"Yes," said Terri, about the tea and biscuits, "we'll have to try to get down to their store, maybe tomorrow. They have all kinds of neat things, along with lots of healthy stuff, too. It's really a fun place. There's lots of neat shops, close by to browse in. Also, in the morning, we'll go to the *Shop n' Stop* to get fresh produce. When I get a chance, I usually try to get to the *Haymarket* but that's only on Fridays and Saturdays. Obviously, this week-end, was a little messed up to make it but we'll go sometime. We'll go visit Jack, my butcher, tomorrow too. You'll like him, he's funny and his shop is great, too. He has a son about your age, I think."

"Terri, it's O.K.," said Brianna, then. "I know what I have to do. My father told me I *should not* go to the police station, tomorrow afternoon. He said, *not to talk to anyone*, until our lawyer gets here. I however, feel differently. I really just want to go in and talk to Captain Mathews and *tell him the truth.*" Brianna took a deep breath and went on. "I see no reason to hold back from telling him what I know, or rather in this case, what I *do not* know. One way or another, it has to come out. They probably can't charge my mom with anything anyway because of her condition. She hasn't been mentally healthy for a long time, at least not as far back as I can remember. I want her to get help and if what she has done to herself, led her to commit a murder, then it can be a lesson for everyone else. Also, there is certainly a very good chance, she *did not* murder Ed. I hope they are able to prove that someone else did, anyway." She finished with a heavy, exhausted, sigh.

"You know Brianna, I can't believe I have only known you for a few days. I guess that's how it is, when so much has happened." Terri sighed, too and finally just plain ran out of steam. "Let's get some sleep. Can you be up by 8:00?" Brianna assured Terri she could. "O.K., set your alarm and we'll start fresh in the morning. We have a lot to do before noon and if you are sure you can handle it, we had better be at the police station, by or well before, 1:30. That's what Captain Mathews told me, when he called this morning."

Brianna hadn't lost her sense of humor, however worried she might be because at the mention of Rico, she said, "Mmmm, so *he called*, huh? I didn't know that. Any chance *he* may have been calling for something *besides* business or does he continue to be a mystery man?" Brianna couldn't help grinning a little, even as tired as she was.

"Yeah, *mystery man,* that's a good handle for this guy," said Terri, as she moved to clean up the tea things. Brianna followed her into the kitchen. Maria had managed to bat a soft, sparkly ball, cat toy out from under one of the counters and she and Louie were chasing it around, under the table. "No, the only reason he called was to set up the appointment. Nothing else but I'm not giving up hope, yet," Terri finished, trying not to sound too discouraged.

"That's good, you never know," said Brianna to this and then, she noticed the two busy felines. "Aren't they something?" she asked, watching them play. "They don't care what's going on out in this stupid world, with stupid humans and their stupid annoying problems. Life is so simple for them. Eat, sleep, use the litter box, sleep some more, play, eat some more, litter box again, play and sleep, that's their day."

"Yeah, well, that's why we keep them as pets or do they keep us? I have yet to figure out that age old question, especially when it comes to cats," Terri commented, as they put their few dishes into the dish washer. She then told Brianna to go ahead and take the bathroom first.

By the time they settled in, they were both so tired, getting to sleep would be no problem. Louie and Maria, were totally confused as to where they should sleep, as they always slept with Terri. The problem was solved when, on her own, Maria settled in with Brianna and Louie took his usual spot by Terri. Noises prevailed outside, on the busy streets of Boston but with the low hum of the air-conditioning and fatigue overcoming them, Terri and Brianna, both slept peacefully.

Chapter 18

The next morning, the girls were at the *'Stop 'n Shop'* by 8:45. No time or need, for glamour, they had both quickly showered, dressed and headed out in Terri's truck. Brianna loved riding in the truck. She enjoyed being in a working environment and appreciated the benefits of getting things done, especially for other people. She had been involved with selfish people for as long as she could remember and it had nearly ruined her life. Of course, Brianna was still very much concerned for her mother. She was determined however, not to let it interfere with the work she had promised Terri she would do. It was like she was getting a fresh start, in a whole new world. For this morning, it was the wonderful, colorful and bright new world of fresh produce.

"This place is awesome!" Brianna exclaimed. This was another part of everyday life, she had never been exposed to. All the groceries, for her household, had been delivered right to the door. On rare occasion, for entertaining purposes, Louise had been obligated to go on shopping trips, for special items. Brianna had never been allowed to go on these excursions, however. *'Let the servants to it, it's their job,'* her mother had always said, when Brianna had begged to go along. That had never sounded correct, to Brianna. Somewhere deep inside, as young as she was back then, she had known this was not the right way to treat other people. It wasn't that her mother had abused Louise and Annette, or treated them like slaves, but she had never been kind or appreciative. Maybe she couldn't help it but Brianna never found any reason to excuse her mother's behavior. She should have known better a long time ago and corrected it. They had wasted a lot of time, it seemed. For now anyway, Brianna finally had a chance to do what she had always wanted to do, shop and cook. This meant, working hard and she was looking forward to it.

Terri loaded up their cart, with fresh spinach, celery, red onions, cabbage, sweet corn, baby carrots, broccoli, and bright, white mushrooms. She was going to make cabbage leaves, filled with a cheese and vegetable stuffing, and pork chops, with a bread stuffing. She had dried bread cubes, back at the restaurant, so that was covered. Terri also, had her own shelf of spices and herbs but she needed more basil, paprika and cumin. Terri always bought herbs and spices in bulk and filled her own large containers. It was not only economical but practical. She saved money and always had the spices, she used the most, on hand. They also grabbed large containers of sour cream and condensed milk, along with noodles to cook, for the stroganoff.

Terri also found a good deal on cream soups, so she bought a case each of cream of chicken and cream of mushroom. Kept in a cool, dry place, the soups would keep longer, than it would take Terri to use them.

"Always look for deals," Terri told Brianna. "I check grocery adds in the newspapers, every week-end. One odd thing I have noticed over the years, as I've worked for different people is, even rich people, at least the smart ones anyway, like to get stuff on sale. It's kind of a psychological thing. I don't imagine Donald Trump thinks about it much but I would bet you, when some of these movie star moms shop, incognito of course, they like to get bargains, just as much as anyone else."

All these little buying tips, fascinated Brianna and she wanted to learn everything at once.

"Information overload, be careful," Terri laughed, as she wrote out a check for their groceries. "To quote one of my favorite movie lines, *'we learn by doing.'* It will all come with time. Let's head for the butcher shop next. Time for you to meet Jack. You'll love his place and we have stuff to pick-up there."

They stopped quickly at the butcher shop. Terri needed to pick-up the cheeses that she had ordered, see if Jack had any special deals for her and introduce him to Brianna. Jack was delighted for Terri and asked her if any progress had been made in the Ed Stone murder case. Of course, it hadn't but Jack knew Terri was involved and she appreciated his genuine concern. He was a good friend, not just a business acquaintance. So much had changed in just the week, from when she had last seen him. For Terri though, along with the bad, there had been much good and the best had been finding her new assistant.

"You have been needing someone to help you for a long time," Jack remarked. "Nice to meet you Brianna," he said, as they shook hands.

"Got a good deal for you today, Terri," he then said, as Terri looked at Brianna and grinned.

"I thought you might," she said, "along with my cheeses, of course. So what else have you for got me?"

"Lamb chops, trimmed off the bone and they aren't going to get priced any lower. If you think you can use them, I can give you a great deal, on five pounds or more." After telling her the price, Terri decided on ten pounds. She could put the lamb into the freezer, until next week, as she had her meals planned and the meats out, for this week. She and Brianna also picked up Monterey Jack, cheddar and mozzarella cheeses. Terri told Brianna, a few things about cheese.

"My cousin, Courtney, lives in Wisconsin and she has worked with cheese and she has sent me cheese," Terri explained. "What most places call Monterey Jack, is no more than a mild brick. When it comes to cheddar, you have to really watch quality. Mild to medium cheddar, is excellent for cooking, for melting, shredding for tacos, that kind of thing. To get a really, sharp cheddar, you have to know what to look for. I *really* love sharp cheddar with some taste, some bite, the older, the better. An 8-year old cheddar can cost at much as $13.00 a pound but it's worth it! A good sharp cheddar, is firm and lighter in color, than medium or mild. It can't even really be sliced or melted. It just comes off the knife in chunks, so yummy, with a glass of good wine," she said, and thinking of other terrific choices with wine, Terri went on. "Oh, there is nothing better, than a really good Brie. Also, there is goat cheese, gouda, gruyere, the list goes on and on. Of course, when you are of legal drinking age, that will be your choice but learning about wines, is a must when you are in the business of serving food." Terri wrote out another check for their purchases, as Brianna examined some of the specialty wines Jack sold at his store.

Terri watched Brianna and felt a great deal of satisfaction. She noticed her soaking up her surroundings with genuine interest and taking in every word her new boss said. This girl was intelligent and then some. Brianna was missing nothing and Terri knew she would be a quick study. Terri could never figure out what was more difficult. Learning a new job or training someone for a new job. However, since Brianna knew quite a bit about food and cooking already, Terri had a feeling the training process would go pretty smoothly, for both of them.

They arrived at *Twin Pines* at about 10:30, with their arms full of bags of fresh veggies, cheeses, the lamb chops and a few miscellaneous items. Terri had grabbed a couple of new knives for Brianna to use, a couple of packages of wooden spoons, for stirring and a large package of plastic spoons, for tasting. Any sampling of foods, was done with a plastic spoon, which was then thrown away, for sanitary reasons. They also brought in the cases of cream soups and stored them in the large basement, on one of the dry goods shelves.

Then they finally put on plastic gloves and got down to work. Terri, quickly put water on to boil for noodles, to go with the beef stroganoff. Brianna wanted to try her hand at planning one of the meals herself and Louise had taught her how to make this traditional dish. This meal could be teamed with a salad, or fresh fruit and rolls.

Dustin had put the prime ribs in the oven yesterday for her, where they had cooked slowly, during the day. He had then placed them in the refrigerator, last night. She now took them out and Brianna watched, as using a sharp, shiny carving knife, Terri sliced the three roasts into enough slices, to fit each family. She sliced equal portions for each person, children and adults. Most of the young ones, of Terri's clients, were old enough to handle a knife and fork. There was never any food left over, as far as she knew. Whatever the kids didn't eat, the grown-ups did. Along with the succulent slices of beef prime rib, Terri would add an au jus, twice baked potatoes, and baby carrots. This could possibly, serve as a Sunday meal. Of course, Terri never questioned *or wondered* for that matter, when her clients, decided to eat which meal. She did, however, get plenty of feedback, helping her decide how to plan their meals.

The water for the noodles was boiling, so Brianna watched, as Terri put ten cups of uncooked pasta into the huge pot. When the noodles were cooked and drained, Terri would put them aside. They browned chunks of tender beef, with flour, salt and pepper and onions. Brianna prepared a wonderful sauce, with sour cream, the spices of her choosing and the fresh, white mushrooms. The sauce was delicious and got Terri's enthusiastic approval. After browning and cooking the beef, it would be put over the noodles, and the sauce poured into separate containers, to be warmed and added before serving. They also added bright, green pieces of steamed broccoli, on the side.

For the other two meals, Terri made chicken breasts, stuffed with steamed spinach and 'Jack' cheese. Brianna helped her mix-up stuffing, cut an incision, in each thick pork chop and fill them with the sage, celery and bread mixture. With the chicken, they made cheesy potatoes and added the stuffed cabbage. To go with the pork, they made gravy and instant mashed potatoes, and then added the buttery, fresh corn.

Brianna had lots of experience, for starts. She had chopped celery and onions and helped pre-cook the cabbage leaves. She had browned the pork chops and flattened the chicken breasts. They had boiled the fresh sweet corn and cut the milky, white nibs off the cobs. She had also made the sauce, for the stroganoff and helped Terri with the other sauces and gravies. Terri had advised her on how to make the meals look, as well as, taste good and taught her how to place portions, equally in each of the sixteen, meal containers. Gravy and au jus, were also put in separate containers. This Terri did, with any sauces or gravies, that went with her meals. These, like the sauce for the stroganoff, would be thawed, reheated and added, to meats or vegetables.

They really had to hustle to get everything cooked, roasted, steamed and baked. By the time they had done all the cleaning up and the meals were prepared and portioned out into the containers, ready for delivery, Terri saw that it was 1:00.

"Oh man, I'd better get a hold of Angie," said Terri, as she saw the time, "there is no way we can get the meals delivered and make it to the police station by 1:30."

Not surprisingly, at this point, Terri's cell rang and it was, ta-da, none other than Angie.

"You aren't going to believe this one!" Angie started the conversation, in her usual, *'everything is screwed up'* way. "Rico got called out on a case. At least this time, it wasn't some *mysterious family emergency*. He's been working on this one for awhile and needed to go check out a lead. I do, however, have some news on the gun." Angie hesitated for a second. "Is Brianna with you?"

"Yes, of course she is. We are just getting ready to put everything in the truck, so I was going to call you. I'm relieved, as usual, that we have more time." Terri glanced at Brianna. "You have news for me?"

"Yeah," said Angie, "and it really doesn't mean much. They found the gun. Actually, someone's dog found it in a park, in some bushes, which happens more than you realize. I love it when they scare the crap out of their owners, by digging guns and knives and stuff, out of shrubbery," Angie laughed.

"Angie, would you get on with it, please?" Terri saw Brianna's questioning look and needed to know what was happening, if Angie would ever actually tell her anything.

"Yeah, sorry. Anyway, turns out the gun was stolen. Surprise, surprise. It had dog slobber and dirt, all over it but they still might be able to find some prints. Who knows? Not my area of expertise." Angie finished her news.

Terri had sighed with relief, at this information. Although she wasn't exactly sure what it meant, she quickly told Brianna.

"Oh, and keep this under your hats, you guys," Angie cautioned. "Obviously, my Captain, still is not aware of the fact, that we have no idea, where the unstable Elizabeth was, on the night of the murder. So, until he talks to Brianna, we have to keep this all just amongst the three of us, got it?"

"Got it, Sherlock!" Terri quipped.

"Yeah, the same to you, Nancy Drew," Angie fired back, "I'll call you later. Signing off!"

"Oh brother," said a once more exasperated Terri, "sometimes I'm amazed that they let *her* carry a gun."

"Seriously?" Brianna looked shocked and then Terri laughed.

"No, I'm totally kidding. She's a terrific cop. Pretty looney sometimes but she's always been like that, so looney person, looney cop. Mmmmm, anyway, we have another reprieve, as it were. Captain Mathews is out on another case and we have to get these meals delivered." Terri picked up a stack of containers and Brianna did the same, as they went out to the truck.

"This is really getting bizarre," said Brianna. "As I have been waiting to talk to Captain Mathews, I have been hoping, this stupid case would get solved and I won't have to tell him, about my mother. She's so screwed-up, that I am sure she will not remember where she was or what she did. Or, if she does remember, there is no way she is going to *fess-up!* I have seen and heard her lie a million times. She's a real pro, at it."

Terri looked at Brianna sympathetically, with no comment. There really was no way to reassure this girl, that everything was going to be O.K. All they could do, was carry on with their work and see what would happen next.

Terri took Brianna to all of the homes where she left meals and showed her the procedure. She had an impressive set of keys, for back doors and freezers, each marked or colored coded, to go with each house. There were notes at each home, instructing a meal be left out for the evening, along with Terri's check. As usual, she left a tentative menu, for the next week. Brianna's eyes bugged out when she saw the checks.

"This is a very lucrative business, I see," she said, "and I can also see how having an assistant, will help you expand. Hey, Terri," Brianna said, then suddenly inspired, "you really should have your own place, with stoves and freezers and refrigerators, the whole bit. Let me buy you a place, man we could really go somewhere with this!" She grabbed Terri and startled her in the process.

"Whoa, whoa, take it easy, Brianna," Terri was amazed at the girl's enthusiasm. "You're only 18 years old, give yourself some time to see if this is what you really want to do. I'm not even sure if this is *what I really want to do.* It's awfully hard work, which is why I was looking for help, when you came along. Let's see how it goes, huh?"

"Yeah, I guess I better settle down, a little. I've just never had a job before and I'd love to own a business. I've got all this stupid money, I may as well do something with it. Why not become an entrepreneur? I may be young but I know what I want and more importantly, *what I don't want.* Does that make sense to you, Terri?" Brianna asked, looking at her new boss, anxiously.

"It makes perfect sense." Terri completely agreed and was amazed, once again, at Brianna's insight into how she felt about her life. "One thing at a time, O.K? Let's see if we can get through this one day. We need to get something to eat right now, for us. Let's go to one of my favorite places. It's a deli, they've got everything. You'll love it."

They went to *Susan's Deli Of Course* and had a wonderful, relaxing lunch, even though it was almost 2:30, in the afternoon.

"Do you think Captain Mathews will ever be around to talk to me?" asked Brianna, as she munched on a pickle spear and a chicken salad sandwich.

"I have no idea," said Terri, who had chosen a B.L.T., one of her all-time favorites, with tangy cole slaw. "He certainly is turning into, *Mr. Mysterio*, not to mention, he seems to be constantly, highly in demand. I can't believe that *I* got to talk to him myself and I really don't think I was much help." Terri took a swig of delicious, fruity raspberry, iced-tea and picked up her napkin. Her cell phone rang and she looked at it, before answering. "Whoa, it's Angie, maybe this is something." Terri answered, "Angie, what's going on?"

Suddenly, Brianna's cell went off and Terri looked at her, not believing what she had just heard from Angie. "It's my father," Brianna said, as she saw Terri's shocked face. "Daddy?" she answered and heard the same news Terri had just gotten. "Oh, my God!" Brianna said, her face draining of all color. She and Terri, had both just received, the exact same information, at exactly the same time.

At 1:00, that afternoon, while Terri and Brianna were busy delivering meals to their clients, Brianna's mother, Elizabeth Severson, had checked herself out of the hospital. Having no way to keep Elizabeth there against her will, the hospital could do nothing to make her stay. Elizabeth, it was reported, had called a taxi, gotten into it with the few personal items that were kept in her room and for all intents and purposes, had fallen off the face of the earth.

Chapter 19

Terri and Brianna, tore over to the police station. Brianna's father, David Severson, had everyone out looking, everywhere they could think of, that Elizabeth may have gone. David had given his daughter, a short list of people to call, when Brianna had begged him for something to do. However, so far, anyone she had called had not heard from Elizabeth. Besides, Brianna was convinced now more than ever, that her mother had killed Ed Stone.

"Why, though?" asked Terri, still puzzled by the whole thing. "If you think your mom killed Ed, what would be her motive? How would she have gotten that gun?"

"Geez Terri, I may be quite a bit younger than you but even I know, it's no problem to get a gun," said Brianna, with a shakey voice, "especially if you have money. Anyone can get a gun and if it was stolen, well all the much easier. People walk the streets of New York, selling stolen stuff all of the time. Maybe she got it at a pawn shop, I don't know. Do those guys in pawn shops always know what they're selling? More importantly, do they sell guns, to just anybody?"

"Well, maybe, *hell I don't know!* I haven't been in a pawn shop lately, so you got me there." Terri was totally freaked, by this time. "O.K., fine, so she could easily get a gun. So, what about motive? Did she ever tell you why she hated Ed, so much? Oh, and what about my spaghetti? Would *your mother,* have sat down with Ed, accepted his offer to eat supper with him and then, for some weird reason, shot him?" Terri ran out of steam and stopped for a breath.

"Terri, what the hell are you talking about?" asked Brianna, looking more confused than ever.

Terri looked over at Brianna, who was suddenly looking at Terri, as if her face had just turned green. Maybe it had, she thought, as she glanced in the rear view mirror of her truck. Whew, not yet or rather, not again! They were at the police station and Terri pulled into the back parking lot.

"I'll explain later," she said, "let's see if we can find Angie, before the roof blows off this place!"

"Oh, it will anyway," said Brianna, as they hopped out of the truck and she ran to keep up with Terri. "When Captain Mathews finds out about my Mom disappearing last week too, the roof will definitely blow off of this building and *we* will be under the rubble!"

"O.K., nice allegory," said Terri, "you're catching on. This way," she said, steering Brianna through a door and up two flights of stairs.

They pushed through the door, at the second floor, to just another day at the local cop-shop, a flurry of noise and activity. Angie saw Terri and Brianna immediately and ran over to them. She steered her friends over to her desk and found them chairs. Angie, in full police get-up, always looked imposing, despite her short stature.

"Brianna," she looked first at the younger girl, "did you get any news on your mother?" Brianna stared at Angie, for a few seconds, until Angie grabbed her by the shoulders and shook her out of her stupor.

"No," Brianna answered, flustered and upset, "you?"

"No, nothing, zip, zero," Angie said, and sat back in her chair. She grabbed a handful of tissues and wiped the sweat off of her forehead. "You know," she said, "this should have been the easiest case in the world. Not very smart guy gets into trouble gambling, pisses off bad guys. Pissed off bad guys, waste not very smart guy. Over, done with, case solved.

What the hell are we missing here? Believe me, we tried to trace this back to the places where he hung out, the people he hung out with, neighbors, the mailman, anyone who may have seen something, anything suspicious. *Nothing!* Everything has been a dead end. Now Elizabeth Severson flies the coop and we have a new problem. I, for one, am stumped and wiped out!"

"What I want to know," said Brianna, *totally pissed-off, again,* "is why is she doing this to me?"

"She isn't doing this to you, Brianna," Angie told her firmly, "she's doing this to herself. You are not to blame for any of the bad decisions made by your mother. Don't ever forget that!"

Terri opened her mouth to say something but nothing came out because she looked up and saw Rico, or rather Captain Mathews. He was coming through the door, she and Brianna had just come in. He was striding towards them and he did not look happy. Whatever was on his face, however, did not come out of his mouth. He was as professional and courteous as ever, as he came up to the three women. *Damn him!*

"Hello ladies," Rico addressed them, politely. "I am going to assume, you are all gathered here for the same reason. I am sorry about your mother Brianna and as you can imagine, we need to find her as soon as possible. Do you have any idea, aside from what has already been thought of, where she may have possibly gone?"

Brianna swallowed and Terri could see, she was indeed, nearly ready to blow the roof off of the police station. This situation would have been too much for anyone, much less an inexperienced, 18 year old girl. Brianna, however kept her cool and Terri was proud of her.

"No Sir," she said, calmly. "I have spoken with my father. He gave me a list of some people to call and I got no information from the ones I contacted. I am sorry I can't think of anyone else, at least not at the moment. I want to find my mother, more than anyone, Captain Mathews, as *you* can imagine." Brianna handed Rico the list of people she had called. Even though she seemed calm enough, Terri could see her hands were shaking.

Rico took the piece of paper and glanced at it but since he knew no one on the list anyway, it really didn't help him much.

"Would you be up to answering some questions now, Brianna?" he asked and then had an after thought. "Is it O.K. if I call you Brianna?"

"Of course, that's fine. I don't think anyone has ever called me Ms. Severson, or anything like that, except for teachers of course and I'm not in school, at the moment. Yes, I can answer some questions now. I think this interview has been put off enough times, wouldn't you say?" Brianna grabbed Terri's hand, making Terri realize how nervous she was, despite the cool demeanor.

"Yes, it really is time we got down to it. Angie, could you accompany us, please? Terri, I would prefer you wait here, if that is alright with you." Rico, or apparently, Captain Mathews at the moment, looked at Terri and she cringed. *No, it was not alright with her.* She was very upset, *and she did not want to wait there.* As it was, obviously, there wasn't a damn thing she could do about it, so she just nodded. Terri watched them walk away and around the corner. She was pissed, *really pissed!*

"Terri, I would prefer you wait here...nay, nay, nay..," Terri said out loud in a mocking voice, which, of course was totally ignored by everyone around her. *He would prefer, huh? Well, maybe she did not prefer to wait there and at this point, gorgeous cop or no gorgeous cop, he could just jump off the Longfellow Bridge if he thought he could tell her......*

Suddenly, Terri's cell phone chirped and she jumped out of the chair. She had forgotten she had been clutching it tightly in her hand. *How could she forget?* That's what she normally did. She looked at the caller I.D. and saw that it was Cal. Maybe he had some news about Elizabeth! She quickly answered it and got a lot of static but she could hear Cal, sounding like he was far away or in a closet or something.

"Cal!" Terri screamed getting no response and feeling suddenly, panicky. *Something is definitely wrong,* Terri thought, as she tried to call him back and got more static. She had to get out of this noisy building and get a better signal. At this point, she had to do something besides sit on her hands. *Be careful, Terri,* she cautioned herself. *'Don't go down into the basement with nothing but a lit candle,'* like in some stupid cheesy, horror flick, she thought. She remembered a comedian saying that once, as a joke but it actually made sense. All silly thoughts aside, that was the phrase Terri and Angie used, to describe going into any situation, that was obviously dangerous. Right now, Terri was running out of options.

She looked around for anyone she knew, to leave Angie a message. *Where in the hell was Will?* Probably out in the squad or whatever. They all had stuff going on. The only thing she could think to do, was scribble Angie a quick note, informing her, she had heard from Cal, was heading to his house and to call, as soon as she read the note. Maybe Cal had heard from Elizabeth and was trying to contact someone. All Terri could do was drive to his house and keep trying to contact him.

Terri ran out of the building, as before, getting no notice from the busy people around her. She tried to get Cal back again, but it just rang and rang until some automatic voice-mail kicked in. *What in the hell was going on?* She got her keys out of her pocket and ran to her truck. *Was Cal at his house? Could she assume that?* It wasn't like she could go tearing over there. She'd just end up getting stopped for speeding. She tried Cal again and then wondered if she shouldn't call and interrupt Brianna's questioning. Yeah, that would put her on *Captain Mathew's shit list,* if this turned out to be nothing.

She continued to try to call Cal, as she navigated around corners and stopped at traffic lights. Were none of them going to be green today? *Grrrr...*she felt like she was moving in slow motion, like in some weird movie. *Strange how often, art defined life or was it life defined art? Mmmm,* well, where did people get ideas for movies and books, anyway? Sometimes, plot lines were like real life and more often not. Most times, real life was boring as hell. Terri wished her life was a little more boring, at the moment, as she finally approached Cal's house.

O.K., his green, Buick La Sabre was in the garage. The place looked very quiet and Terri felt the hairs on the back of her neck stand up and a chill go down her spine. *Whoa, that really was like real life!* She definitely felt creepy and alarmed. *Yes, really alarmed.* That was what she was feeling, now. Suddenly, as she looked at her cell phone, still clutched tightly in her hand, Terri had an inspiration. She had just done on upgrade and had the smallest phone she could get, so it would easily fit in a pocket. Right now, she looked at it and changed the ring tone, to *vibrate*. Then she deftly placed the tiny phone in to her bra. Not being all that well-endowed, she hoped it would *stay there*. Fortunately, the particular undergarment she chose that morning, was of the under wire type. The small instrument, fit snuggly between her breasts and rested at the bottom, laying neatly against the wire, in the bra. She could feel the sweat running down her face and she wiped it impatiently away, with some napkins laying on the seat of the truck. She slowly got out of her truck and tried to figure out if someone was in the house. The front door was open and she approached cautiously.

"Cal," she called out and then wished she hadn't. Although, if someone was in the house, *wouldn' t they see her coming anyway?* She walked through the front door and breathed a sigh of relief when she saw Cal, sitting safely in his favorite recliner. The T.V. was on but there was no sound coming from it.

"Terri, you should not have come over here," Cal said, with a strained look of warning.

"You called me, Cal," Terri said. "I knew something was wrong. What is going on?"

"My father is correct," said the voice of Elizabeth Severson, behind Terri, "you should not have come but I knew you would." Terri started to turn around but realized a gun was being pushed into the back of her skull. Not knowing what else to do but feeling calm, she put up her hands and didn't move.

Chapter 20

"Did you kill Ed, Elizabeth?" Terri asked then, trying to sound as cold and angry as this crazy woman behind her. "Is that what this is all about?"

"No, Terri," said Cal. "I killed Ed!"

"What?" Terri could suddenly feel herself losing her composure. "Why? How did this happen?" She moved to go over to her old friend but Elizabeth stopped her.

"Don't move, you little bitch!" Elizabeth screamed. "Daddy, stop! Don't tell her anything. If she tells the police you killed Ed, you will go to jail. Your heart can't take it, Daddy. You'll die in jail. No, we are going to say, that I killed Ed. I certainly had enough reason." She pushed the gun into Terri's head and shoved her forward. "Sit down, you interfering, stupid brat! If you had stayed out of this, we could have settled it on our own. You had to bring my daughter into this. My daughter, you've taken her away from me and now she is going to tell the police, I was gone the night of the murder. Now sit down damn you, next to my father. I have to think."

Terri moved forward but Elizabeth stopped her. "Wait," she said, "where is your damn cell phone? You girls always have your stupid phones with you, where is it?"

"I don't know. I mean, I guess it's still in my truck! I must have dropped it on the floor, when I was driving over here," Terri lied, smoothly. At this point, Elizabeth reached down on each side of Terri and checked her pockets. Terri assumed, or hoped, she wouldn't dare check anywhere else.

"Fine," Elizabeth said angrily, "then sit the hell down!"

Terri finally turned around and looked at Elizabeth. She truly appeared to be certifiably insane. Her hair was tangled, her face was red and her eyes were wild, with what appeared to be intense pain. Terri could see a half-full, *or was it half-empty?*, booze bottle on the the table behind Cal's daughter. She was holding a gun, much larger than any hand gun, Terri had ever seen but then she didn't know much about guns. Another stolen piece, bought off the street, perhaps? Seemed a moot point, at this juncture. Terri was in no doubt, that this freaked out woman, knew exactly how to use it and she wasn't of a mind to test her.

Terri suddenly felt her phone vibrating and was grateful, that Elizabeth reached down and took another drink of booze, missing the look on her face. Good, Angie would be alerted and the G.P.S. in Terri's phone would help them find her, if she could just hold Elizabeth off. Terri reached over and took Cal's shaking hand.

"Can I find out what's going on, here?" Terri asked, trying to sound as if she was in charge. Elizabeth was getting pretty plastered but the gun in her hand was still pointed at Terri and Cal.

"Sure, Sweetie," said Elizabeth, in a mocking voice, "because I have every intention of killing you. Why not? They think I'm nuts, anyway, so I'll get off, with an insanity plea and my father will be safe. Oh, and I was the one who called you. I knew you would come, you and you're stupid cop friend. You think you're so damn smart but I'm smarter. Crazy people are smart and cagey, didn't you know that? Go ahead and tell her Daddy, tell her why you shot, your so-called best friend, *that son-of-a bitch!* Tell your little pal, *Terri Springeeeee...*, why the bastard needed to die, to be executed."

"Elizabeth, please put that down gun and stop this." Cal pleaded with his daughter. "You, we are *not* going to kill Terri. That is not going to help us or save me."

Terri, stung more than a little, by the way Elizabeth had just made fun of her last name, looked at Cal gratefully and squeezed his hand.

"Get your hands off of my father!" Elizabeth screamed at her and Terri obligingly let go of Cal's hand. What else could she do to keep this woman from getting any angrier, than she already was? "Who and the hell do you think you are, anyway? You don't even know my father and *you sure as hell did not know, that ass-hole, Ed Stone!"*

Terri said nothing to any of this. She had no reason to doubt, that this hysterical woman, was correct in most of what she was saying. She certainly had not known much about Ed but she definitely was having a difficult time, believing Cal had killed him.

"O.K., little girl," said Elizabeth, slurring her words and taking another drink, "we are going for a ride, the three of us. While your little cell phone is leading the cops, or whoever, over here, we will be driving in a totally different direction. "Let's go, *move!"* She motioned with the gun and Cal, got up from his chair. Terri could see, that he was pale and sweating profusely. Cal stumbled and Terri grabbed his arm. She was concerned he was going to pass out and Elizabeth seemed to take no notice, just another swig of booze.

"Elizabeth!" Terri tried to get her to look at Cal, "your father is ill. We should call an ambulance."

"Oh yeah, sure and have cops all over the place. Give him one of his pills, there in that bottle and he'll be fine. Time to get moving, Terri honey," she said, trying to sound sweet as pie. "You'll be driving Daddy's car and I'll be in the back seat, holding the gun to your head. Now let's go!"

Terri made sure Cal took one of his heart pills, with a drink of water. "I'm fine, Terri," said Cal, "let's go." Then in a low voice he said, "She's drinking an awful lot, let's just try to stall as long as we can."

"Stop talking, damn it! Get going, *now!* Sorry Daddy but in order for me to get rid of this chick, we have to leave this house.

I'm not going to jail and neither are you. I have it all planned, now let's get out of here, before they track her phone."

Speaking of Terri's phone, she felt it vibrating like crazy, next to her skin and prayed they would be tracing the signal to wherever Elizabeth might be taking them. They went outside and got into Cal's car, with Terri driving.

"Now, let's head for the cemetery, where our old buddy Ed Stone, is buried. Do you know where that is, Terri honey?" Elizabeth asked mockingly, pushing the gun into the back of Terri's head.

"Yes, I do know where it is," Terri tried to sound calm. Cal was in the front seat with her and she looked over at him. He did not look well and Terri could feel herself, increasingly concerned for him. She backed the car out and turned right, heading for the cemetery. It was about 15 or 20 minutes away and she had to find out, right now, what the hell this was all about. Her phone was no longer vibrating, leading Terri to believe they were being tracked, so she took a deep breath and started asking questions.

"O.K., so we are heading for Ed's grave. If you think you have to kill me too, Elizabeth, to settle this whole thing, could you at least tell me why Ed Stone deserved to die? How about making it, oh I don't know, like a last request?" Terri tried to sound light and Elizabeth was getting so smashed, Terri was afraid the gun would go off by accident. This was adding to her anxiety, as she tried to drive and not run off the road.

"Fine, oh and just to let you know, the other reason I'm killing you, besides that you know what's going on," Elizabeth started the story casually, like she was talking about the weather, "is that *I want my daughter back!* She's mine and you had this brilliant idea, that has taken her away from me. If I have her back home, where she belongs, I won't have to stay in that stupid hospital. Also, when the cops find you laying on Ed's grave with the gun, they'll just figure it was you who killed the bastard and that let's me and Daddy off! Oh, man, I can't believe how brilliant I am. This is just too fun! I've got it all figured out. So, go ahead Daddy, tell her why you shot your old buddy."

"Elizabeth, whatever happens here, *I will not let you kill Terri*. She has done nothing wrong. She is a good friend and does not deserve to die." Cal was breathing hard and getting more pale.

Terri could hardly concentrate on the road and she was finding it more difficult then ever, to stop from shaking. If Elizabeth didn't have the gun pressed to the back of her head, she could maybe figure out a way to reason with her. Well, whatever *brilliant* plan, Elizabeth thought she had, was in Terri's mind, pretty stupid. *There was no way, she had any intention of letting Elizabeth try to make it appear, as if she, Terri, had shot Ed! Not in this lifetime.* Right now, she had to think of something and fast. In the meantime, Cal was going on with the story.

"For that matter, Ed did not deserve to die either. I had no right to go to his house and pass sentence on him. It was impulsive and wrong. No one has the right to take the life of another human being. I have wished everyday, since it happened, that I had not done it." Cal stopped and continued to breath, heavily.

"After what he did to me, Daddy?" Elizabeth, was wimpering now. Her moods were eratic and her voice had changed pitch, like a little girl. "He raped me Daddy. Tell Terri what he did to me. He raped me, when I was only 17 and then he said, *that I was asking for it.* He said that, *I was a tramp, wearing sexy clothes and flirting with him.* That's not true Daddy, I was not a tramp! He was so nice to me and he was really handsome back then. I had such a crush on him." Elizabeth was crying now but she did not let go of the gun. "I thought he cared about me and then when I told him I was pregnant, he laughed and said, *it wasn' t his, that I had probably had sex with a bunch of other guys.* That was not true! I had never been with anyone else and he was so horrible!"

"Elizabeth, stop this now!" Terri pleaded with her, shocked by her revelations, about Ed. "What happened to you *was horrible.* You can get past this and feel better, someone can help you. *Please,* Cal isn't feeling well. Let's just go and...."

"Shut-up, who said you can talk, anyway?" Elizabeth pushed the gun a little harder into the back of Terri's neck. "Besides, here we are. There's no turning back, honey. Go into the cemetery and drive around to where the grave is."

Terri was starting to feel real fear. *Oh please,* she prayed silently, *please God, let them be on their way.* She drove over to where the fresh grave was and she and Cal got out of the car, with Elizabeth close behind them. She had the gun in Terri's back now and went on with the story.

"After I lost the baby, my baby boy," Elizabeth said, sniffling, "I went to Ed and told him and he was glad. He just kept laughing at me, telling me he was glad the kid was dead. The last thing he needed, *was some damn kid around,* he said, *that is, if it was even his.* Oh yeah, he continued to add that little part. *It probably wasn' t even his kid,* he said and *he was not paying to take care of someone else's stupid brat!*"

"I went over to his house to talk to him about all of this," Cal said, now, "and he still had the same attitude, as Elizabeth said. He showed no remorse or sorrow for what he had done to her. I never knew what had happened. Loretta did but she couldn't handle it, either. She never told me and I continued to believe, that Ed was my friend. We had always done everything together but I just closed my eyes, to all the signs. He was always so selfish, about everything. He always used women and pretty much just about anyone he could and I always defended him. He had saved my life a couple of times, in Korea but hell, we all did that, for fellow soldiers. That's just the way it was over there. It didn't really mean anything, once we got home."

They had gotten to Ed's grave now and stood looking at it. *Where in the hell was her buddy, Pete Richards, who had scared the daylights out of her, when she had been here last week? Not his day to mow lawns, presumably.*

Cal went on but his breathing was getting worse. "I got to Ed's, that night and he was having supper. Your spaghetti,

Terri and so he offered me some. I didn't really know yet, what the whole story was, so I fixed myself a plate, like I had done a hundred times before. We always ate meals together, sometimes at his house, sometimes at mine. You had just been there, it seemed and he was enjoying his food with gusto, as usual, when I asked him about Elizabeth. I don't think I ever even took a bite of mine." Cal wiped the sweat from his brow and got even paler. "He laughed at me, just like he did Elizabeth. He said, *yeah, what a looker she was and that she had asked for it, so he 'gave it to her.'* I still can't believe he said it like that. My daughter was only 17 and Ed acted like it was her fault. He didn't even apologize. He didn't care about what he had done. Just said *that he was glad to get it off of his chest before he died.* I was stunned Terri, that he talked that way about Elizabeth. He had been so good to her, when she was growing up. What was he doing, making her trust him, so he could do this horrible thing to her? I had the gun in my pocket, for protection, mostly. I got up from the table, shot him, cleaned up my dishes and left, without a backward glance. I'm sorry I did it and I'm sorry you got dragged into this." Cal finished and closed his eyes, as if he couldn't say or do anything else.

Terri looked back at Elizabeth and saw, even though she was still holding the gun, she was looking distracted. Terri also saw *something else* and tried not to visibly relax. *Terri saw Rico,* coming towards them, carefully and silently. Looking to her left, she saw another police officer, Will Collins, not far from his Captain. Both men had their firearms drawn and were quickly making their way to the trio by the grave.

Terri also saw Cal, suddenly clutching his chest and falling to his knees.

Then it was all over. Elizabeth went to her father and Rico came up behind her, immediately, taking the gun and emptying the cartridge. Terri sighed with relief. Elizabeth looked at Rico, like she didn't even see him and then at her father. "Daddy?" She was whimpering again, in the child-like voice. "Daddy, no," Elizabeth cried now and fell to her knees beside her father. Cal was on the ground and Terri was stunned, as she looked at Elizabeth, next to her father on the grass, next to Ed's grave. Will was on his radio, calling for an ambulance and to Terri's surprise, Rico was suddenly at her side.

"Terri," Rico said, putting his arm around her and this time, if felt like a little more than a big brother. It made Terri feel, *safe*. She looked at him and then at Cal, on the ground. Will had pushed the hysterical Elizabeth aside and was trying to help Cal. He looked up at Rico and Terri and shook his head. Cal was gone. There had been nothing they could do. Even if they had gotten him to a hospital, it would not have mattered. His heart had given out, maybe even been broken, by his best friend.

Elizabeth had forgotten anyone else was even there. She was holding her father and crying. "Daddy, no, please wake-up Daddy, please. It's going to be O.K., Daddy. We can be together, always, Daddy, please." Elizabeth was sobbing and Terri felt the tears running down her own face. She hadn't even realized she was crying but why wouldn't she be? Terri had loved Cal and what Ed had done, had been unforgivable.

Terri could finally hear sirens in the background. There were suddenly police cars all over the place. Angie came running up to Terri and Rico. Another police woman, grabbed Elizabeth and cuffed her, prompting Cal's distraught daughter, to scream, as they dragged her away from Cal. Paramedics were on Cal, in an instant, trying, with no avail, to revive him.

Terri turned to look at Rico and realized, she was in some semblance of shock. She started to shake and sob, losing control. Terri felt her knees give out and she dropped to the ground. Rico went down with her and put his arms around her. "Terri, it's O.K., it's O.K.," he said, soothingly and then in the direction of the paramedics, he yelled, "Hey, guys, I need some help here. This lady is suffering from shock. Angie, help me," Rico said. Angie was on the grass, next to Terri and a paramedic came up, with a cool bottle of water and a cloth for her forehead. Terri looked at all of them, and smiled through her tears. "Thank-you, I'm fine," she said, and then, suddenly realizing, how close she came to getting shot, promptly passed out.

Chapter 21

Two months later, on a gorgeous October day, Terri, Angie, and Brianna were sitting in Terri's apartment and as usual, Louie and Maria, were trying to monopolize all the attention. Since there were three girls, however, neither one of them had any reason to feel neglected. So after much coddling, they went off to their bowls and to look for more interesting ways, to get into mischief. The girls had been talking about everything that had happened. After Cal's funeral, Brianna's mother had gone back to the hospital. The fate of the *Mickey Mantle rookie,* baseball card, was yet to be decided but it more than likely, would be donated to a museum. The decision was being left up to a judge.

Terri and Rico had also, slowly but surely, been trying to establish a relationship based on being pals, who occasionally went to a movie or out for coffee. Terri was in no rush and Rico's busy life, left little time for socializing. Terri was very busy too but she still hoped, some day, they might be more than just friends. *'Just friends' yuck,* she hated that term. *Oh, well.* She still didn't know much about Rico, or what was happening in his life, that so often took him away, at a moment's notice. Terri felt, until he could get to know her and trust her enough, to let him into his life, things were fine the way they were.

Right now, she was enjoying a Saturday afternoon with her two best women friends. As usual, they had all had an insane week and they were bumming. They were having a late lunch, of sliced, chicken breast sandwiches, pickles, dill, of course, and fresh veggies with dip. Cold sodas rounded out their meal.

"Man, it's beautiful out," said Terri, as they finished eating. She had opened the bay windows, to let in the gorgeous Fall breezes. Now Louie and Maria jumped up on the window seat, to smell outside smells and listen to the birds. The colors of the trees were beautiful golds, oranges, reds and yellows. It really was a lovely day, in the New England states but the girls knew winter was on the way. Winter in Boston and New York, could be pretty brutal but they were all used to it.

"I can't believe it's been two months already, since my grandfather died and all that other terrible stuff happened," Brianna said, as they sat and enjoyed the lovely autumn weather. "It turned out to be pretty bizarre. I still can't imagine, that Grandpa could kill Ed, no matter what he had done. It just didn't seem to be in his nature. I miss him so much but I can't blame him for what he did. Ed Stone must have been a terrible person." Brianna sighed, as she thought about her grandfather *and* her mother.

"People do a lot of things, on impulse, which can be a good thing, when you decide to put your cell phone in your bra," said Angie, looking at Terri, with a grin. "More often then not though, that's how murders happen. Not many are all that well planned out. If Cal had not been carrying the gun with him, as he told Terri, for protection, he probably would have just left Ed's house, and who knows? Maybe he would have even turned Ed in to the authorities. It certainly explained a lot about your mom though, Brianna and I'm only sorry you had to go through it all." Angie finished, looking out at the gorgeous day, like Terri, with a heavy sigh.

"No one could have known what had happened to my mother. I blame my Grandma Loretta for that," said Brianna, bitterly. "She was, how can I say this, *not a nice woman*. I was only something like, eight years old, when she died but I can't ever remember her having anything good to say about anyone.

Grandpa just put up with her. My mother however, always seemed to be angry with her about something. At least, now I know what it was. No wonder my mother was so freaked out all the time. The older she got, the more booze she had to drink and the more pills, she had to take, to forget what Ed had done to her."

"Also, when we add to the problem what men say, when they commit that kind of a crime against a woman, it just makes it more devastating for the victim," Terri put in. "Rape is not an act of passion brought on by the person, who is assaulted, or by the way someone acts or dresses. Rape is a crime of violence, a way to exert power over someone else. Not only did Ed commit this terrible crime against your mother, Brianna. He also made her pregnant and probably caused her to lose the baby because of the trauma, she had been through."

"Well, knowing I may have had another older brother, is kind of weird," said Brianna, then. "The fact that she married my Dad is pretty strange though, too. I guess she felt like his money and position, would protect her somehow. I've talked to my father about it and he says, she never told him. How could she keep it to herself, all these years?"

"Who knows?" asked Angie. "All the drinking and the drugs, helped her block it all out. Do you think, maybe?"

"Yeah, I guess. She is doing a little better, since it all came out. I have no idea how long she'll be in the hospital. It's the best, of course, that my dad can pay for, so if they can't help her, no one can." Brianna tried to sound hopeful, with little success.

"They will help her, Brianna," Terri said, "and in the meantime, you or rather we, have lots of work to do. Now, that we have taken on four more families and started making party trays, we can hardly keep up."

"Yeah, good thing you agreed to let me put money into a place of our own, yes?" Brianna grinned and Terri shook her head.

"I can't believe you talked me into it but how could we possibly turn down the location?" Terri rolled her eyes, thinking about their good fortune.

How was it, that the building, right next to Amber and Kellie's store, suddenly became available? Terri had her suspicions about it but decided to leave it go. Terri and Brianna's business was growing by leaps and bounds, so much so, they were looking for at least two more people. Terri had given her notice at *Twin Pines* and she and Brianna, had worked to fix up the front room of the building, *all courtesy of Daddy's money,* as Brianna put it. Terri, however, always concerned about proper business practices, had seen to it, that the appropriate papers were drawn up and signed and a loan set-up. The way the business was going, they would have David Severson paid back in no time. In the meantime, Terri was satisfied everything was being done legally and correctly.

"Oh, Angie, by the way," Terri decided to bug her friend, a little bit. "what do you think of the White Sox in the Series, now?"

"Oh, shut-up!" Angie kicked at Terri, good naturedly. "Well, there's always next year."

"I've got a better idea, anyway," said Terri, then, "how about we take Brianna to the Patriot's game, this week-end?"

"Oooo, I'm all up on that," said Brianna, "to the Three Musketeers," she said, raising her soda, "all for one.....

.....and one for all!" the three girls said, together.

"*Oh yeah,*" said Terri, "24 starts in January. Kiefer Sutherland is so hot!"

"What is 24, again?" asked Brianna.

"Well," said Angie, "you see, 24 hours in the life of Jack Bauer....."

"Oh, don't even start," said Terri as she fell back on to the sofa. At that point, Louie, with absolutely no warning, flew over the top and jumped on her head.

"Well," said Terri, untangling the fuzzy feline from her hair, "at least we're getting back to normal."

Brianna laughed then and grabbed Louie, as Maria got up onto the couch and joined in on the fun. Terri and Angie, just looked at each other and smiled.

Terri and Emily Springe's Canned Tomatoes

Terri <u>definitely</u> prefers to use her canned tomatoes but for those who do not have access or the resources to can their own, canned stewed tomatoes (from your favorite market or grocery store) can be substituted. The texture will be noticeably different and more spices may need to be added, to achieve the flavor you want.

One bushel of ripe tomatoes (cut away any bruises or soft parts)
Green Peppers (2 large)
Onions (2 large)
Celery (4 ribs-optional)
Salt, to taste, possibly ¼ to½ cup (taste, as you add)
<u>One tablespoon each:</u>
Black Pepper
Garlic Salt (or fresh garlic, about 6 to 8 toes)
Oregano or Italian seasoning
(spices can be adjusted, to your taste)

Terri and her mom, use the *'open-kettle'* method of canning tomatoes. The high amount of acid, in tomatoes, makes this safe. Also, make sure jars, lids and rings, are piping hot, (some homemakers, put jars through the hot rinse of the dishwasher). Your tomatoes will seal fast and stay sealed. Always use new lids and rings!!! Jars, should be sparkling clean, with no chips or nicks, around the rim of the jar. Scald tomatoes, on top of stove in boiling water. Take care not to get burned! Taking tomatoes, a few at a time, dip into hot water, wait 45 seconds or so. Move scalded tomatoes, using a slotted spoon, to sink full of cold water. After scalding all tomatoes, you will easily be able to remove peelings and cut out core; discard peelings and cores.

In large pot on top of stove, place peeled tomatoes, cut into pieces, along with diced onions, diced green peppers, salt, pepper and other spices.

Boil tomatoes for at least an hour, turning down to medium heat and stirring often. Cook up vegetables, into a stewed tomato mixture. Using rubber gloves, to protect hands, scoop cooking tomatoes, out of pot, into hot jars. Wipe off any excess liquids, around rim of jar. Using cooking tweezers (the kind you would use to turn foods, when grilling), remove hot lids, from sauce pan of simmering clean water, place on rim of jar. Carefully turn on hot lid. Carefully, set filled jar off to side and wait to hear the pop, of a sealed jar of canned tomatoes!! Admire your work and put date on lids.

Spaghetti With Meatballs

Yes, even after Ed's murder, Terri still makes her famous spaghetti with meatballs. No sense crying over spilled sauce. Remember, any reference in recipes to canned tomatoes, can be replaced with stewed tomatoes, bought at the grocery store. This recipe is for a large pot of sauce, with meatballs.

The Sauce (start before making meatballs)

2 quarts of canned tomatoes
1 quart of tomato juice (either bought at store, or puree canned tomatoes, in blender and run through a sieve, disposing of seeds and leftover pulp)
1- 8 oz. can of tomato paste (rinse can, and fill w/water, add to sauce)
1- 8 oz. can of tomato sauce (rinse can, and fill w/water, add to sauce)
1- 4 oz. can of mushrooms (stems & pieces, or fresh, if you have them) salt and pepper (to taste)
2 tsps. garlic salt
2 tsps. oregano

Put all ingredients in large soup pot. Cook sauce, until boiling. Terri always sprays the bottom of the pot with cooking spray and stirs the sauce often. When the sauce starts to boil, turn heat down, so that sauce cooks slowly, for at least 4 hours. Continue to stir often, to prevent sticking.

S. Kay Weber

Meatballs

2 lbs. of ground beef
1 lb. of fresh ground pork
3 large eggs
1 medium onion, diced
2% milk, enough to make mixture moist to roll into 1 inch meatballs
1 cup of bread crumbs, plain or seasoned (or crushed saltines or other plain crackers, crushed. *Do not* throw away crackers, that are no longer crisp, you can use them in meatballs or meatloaf)
2 or three toes of garlic (optional but garlic makes everything taste better)
2 tsp. salt
1 tsp. pepper

Get yourself a large glass, bowl. Mix together, ground beef, pork, eggs, diced onion and bread crumbs. Mix thoroughly, with very clean hands, (or wear plastic gloves), to evenly combine ingredients. Add salt, pepper, garlic (put peeled garlic toes, through garlic press or smash with flat side of large knife) and add milk to make mixture moist enough to form into meatballs. Spray glass cake pan, with cooking spray, place meatballs in pan, as you are forming them. Cook meatballs in 350 degree oven, until completely browned, usually about 45 minutes. Place browned meatballs into sauce and stir thoroughly, to mix into cooking sauce. Your sauce should be getting thicker by now. Carefully taste, don't burn your tongue! Adjust seasonings to your taste.

Serve sauce with meatballs, over angel hair pasta, which Terri prefers, or any other pasta of your choosing. Serve with garlic bread, salad, drinks or a good wine.

This amount of sauce can feed up to 10 people.

Oven 'Fried' Chicken

2 Fryer Chickens (cut into serving pieces)
*(Or, if you prefer, thighs and legs, which are great for picnics, about 5 lbs.)
2 cups of flour
1/3 cup of corn starch
½ cup of bread crumbs (plain or seasoned, do not substitute crackers, for this recipe)
2 tsp. poultry seasoning
2 tsp. garlic salt
1 Tbls. oregano
2 tsp. paprika
1 large egg
1 ½ cups milk
Oil, for browning on top of stove.
Cooking spray to coat pans, for oven.

Put all <u>dry</u> ingredients into zip-loc bag, or plastic container with cover. Mix egg and milk in medium glass, bowl. Dip chicken pieces, one at a time, into milk and egg mixture. Place pieces 2 or 3 at a time, into flour mixture. Shake bag or plastic container, to thoroughly coat chicken pieces, shaking off excess flour mixture. Brown on top of stove in frying pan, in hot oil. Place browned pieces of chicken, in glass, cake pans, coated with cooking spray. Bake in 350 degree oven, for at least an hour, or until juices run clear, and chicken comes apart easily. Drain on heavy, paper towels, placed on cookie sheets. Serve with potatoes of your choice, a salad or California blend vegetables, with cheese sauce. Yummy with another good wine, also of your choice or good, cold beer. Chicken can also be served cold for leftovers or picnics, with cheese, and fruit.

*Note: If you prefer, this recipe is excellent, made with just the drumsticks and thighs, especially for picnics. (Always make sure you refrigerate leftover chicken, to cool properly. Never put warm pieces of chicken in a picnic basket, especially <u>never</u> in aluminum foil.) Packages of just thighs and drumsticks, can often be found, at your favorite grocery or market, on sale!!

Old Fashioned Meatloaf

1 lb. of ground beef
½ lb. of ground pork
1 medium onion
1 cup of old-fashioned oats, dry (don't cook) or bread crumbs
2 medium eggs
Canned tomatoes (enough to moisten ingredients, about 1 to 1½ cups)
Salt and pepper (about 2 tsp. each)
1 tbsp. of vegetable oil (for cooking onions)
1- 4oz. can tomato sauce
Cooking spray to coat pan.

Dice onion and cook until translucent, in small frying pan, on top of stove with about 1 tbsp. of oil. Mix together all ingredients, except tomatoes, again with your hands and add cooked onions. Add tomatoes, enough to moisten mixture. Spray square, glass cake pan with cooking spray and pat mixture into pan. Pour can of tomato sauce over uncooked, meatloaf. Bake at 350 degrees, for at least an hour and a half. Serve slices of this marvelous, moist meatloaf with cheesy or baked potatoes, green beans or fresh cooked baby carrots. This recipe should easily feed 5or 6 people.

Pork Loin Roast

Pork Loin 6-8 pounds
Salt and Pepper, whole loin, thoroughly.
Sprinkle Rosemary (dried or fresh) over top of pork.

Roast at 450 degrees for one hour. Turn oven down to 350 degrees and roast for two more hours. Check your roasted pork, with meat thermometer. Temperature should read, anywhere from 160-170 degrees. Slice into, ¼ inch slices or thicker, if you wish. Serve with mashed potatoes and gravy and fresh vegetables.

This simple recipe, will give you succulent slices of pork and it is also wonderful, served with sour kraut, for a buffet. Lay slices of pork in a flat roasting pan or metal cake pan and layer sour kraut with juice, over top.

(Sour kraut can be purchased at your grocery or market, either canned or in bags, in the deli or meat department.) Warm in oven with meat, to thoroughly heat kraut. Moist and delicious, served with other foods, on the buffet, or in sandwiches, for a quick meal.

This wonderful recipe, was given to me, by my friend and wonderful chef, crusty but soft-hearted, Edward (Ned) Hagen. I miss you Ned!

Teaser (from the author)

Recipes to be featured in my next book, DOUBLE TRUFFLE!

Ouik Chicken Curry Divan (with broccoli)
'The best' **Chocolate Chip Cookies** in The Whole World
Hamburger Noodle Hot Dish (basic family recipe)
Slow-Cooker Beef Stew
Scramble Eggs with TRUFFLES!
…..and that's just for 'starts'
Thanx, for reading, SPAGHETTI WITH MURDER!

Printed in the United States
121373LV00003B/9/A

9 781425 947309